"Seven at one blow!" That's what they say about the Brave Little Tailor—he killed seven giants with one blow. But no one can prove it's even true. And besides, that took place a long time ago, and the Brave Little Tailor is now an old man. So what happens when an army of angry trolls invades his kingdom?

Don't miss these other Further Tales:

The Thief and the Beanstalk

The Eye of the Warlock

The Brave Apprentice

P. W. CATANESE

ALADDIN PAPERBACKS
NEW YORK   LONDON   TORONTO   SYDNEY

The Brave Apprentice

🫖ALADDIN PAPERBACKS
An imprint of Simon & Schuster Children's Publishing Division
1230 Avenue of the Americas, New York, NY 10020
Text copyright © 2005 by P. W. Catanese
All rights reserved, including the right of reproduction
in whole or in part in any form.
ALADDIN PAPERBACKS and colophon are registered
trademarks of Simon & Schuster, Inc.
Designed by Tom Daly
The text of this book was set in Adobe Jenson.
Manufactured in the United States of America
First Aladdin Paperbacks edition July 2005
4   6   8   10   9   7   5   3
Library of Congress Control Number 2004109869
ISBN 0-689-87174-0
1212 OFF

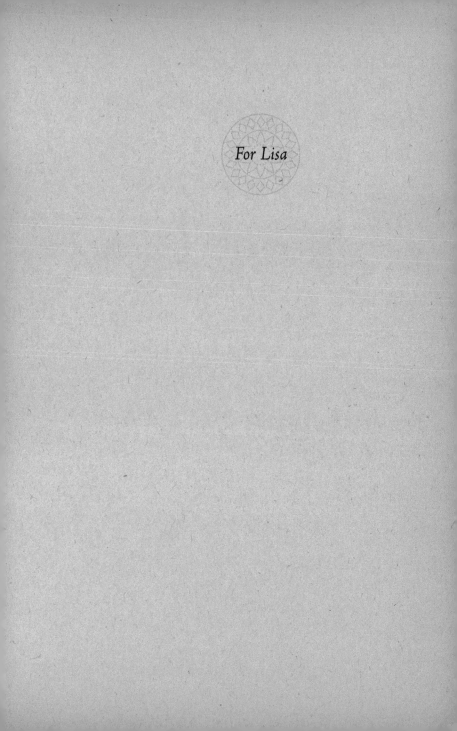

For Lisa

CHAPTER 1

"Look, there's another one."

The tailor squinted at the grassy land on the other side of the river from the village of Crossfield, where a lone sheep had wandered into view with no shepherd or dog in sight.

"I don't like it," he said to the apprentice by his side. "I'm afraid something has happened to old Osbert. Stubborn fool, I told him he didn't look well. Never should have gone out there with the herd."

"I'll find him, master."

"You're a good lad, Patch. Go on, now—there's not much daylight left. And cross the second bridge, mind you, no sense taking chances at the Tumbles." The tailor shouted the last few words because the boy was already running along the footpath by the river's edge.

Patch could run fast and forever, as everyone in town knew. He ran everywhere on those long colt legs, with his tangle of black hair flapping behind him like

1

a pennant. Even when there was no cause to run, Patch ran. But there was a reason now. Earlier that afternoon one of Osbert's sheep had ambled into town unattended. And now this one had appeared across the river. It seemed that neither Osbert nor his dog was minding the flock. Besides, the old shepherd should have been back by now, at the little house next to the tailor's home, with his herd safe in its pen.

The river was running swiftly too, as it always did in spring when the snows melted in the hills of the Barren Gray. As Patch raced along the bank he tried to guess why Osbert had lost track of time and sheep. He hoped the old man had fallen asleep on a sun-warmed rock or was helping one of his flock give birth. But darker explanations tugged at the boy's thoughts, and he dreaded coming at last upon his friend's cold body, somewhere on the other side of the river.

The Tumbles were coming up. Here the banks of the river stood tall and close on each side, and the waters narrowed and hastened between them, frothing among the boulders that cluttered the riverbed. Aging willows lined the banks, and their roots reached into the swirling currents like long probing fingers. The Tumbles bridge was here. It was a simple construction, with wide, sturdy planks nailed along the trunks of two trees that spanned the gap, and no railing on either side. It was a way that few dared to take these days, even though it spared the traveler a long walk to the next bridge much farther downstream. As for Patch, he crossed here often (at least when the sun was shining), sometimes just for the thrill of it.

He took the bridge the same way as always, slowing only a little as he approached the first plank. Then he jumped high, a leap that carried him halfway across. He landed, took two more long steps, and then leaped again to soar over the far end, out of the reach of any large and ugly hand that might dart out grasping from the shadowy place under the span.

Patch stopped and turned to look back at the crossing. No such hand had appeared. But in a strange way, he almost wished that it had. As horrifying as it might be, Patch hoped that one day he might catch a glimpse of the troll that was rumored to live under that bridge.

Between two enormous rocks on the far side was the dark space where the troll had supposedly carved itself a cave just a few months before. No villager had yet gotten a good look at the creature. Once the farmer Dale came puffing white-faced into town, shouting that something had snatched three of his geese as he crossed the Tumbles. People spoke of unearthly groans and a hulking shape glimpsed in the moonlight. And everyone could smell the foul, foul stench that poured from that hole like vapor from a hot spring, the scent of things rotten and dead.

Patch ran to the first hilltop on the far side of the river and stopped to look about. He shouted "Osbert!" three times and held his breath to listen for a reply. None came from his old friend. But somewhere to the north, over the next hill, a dog barked.

He ran with his fists clenched and his thin legs slicing through the knee-high weeds, and when he crested the next hill he saw the shepherd.

Osbert was sitting slumped with his back against a boulder, rocking gently. His head drooped and his chin rested on his chest. His dog, Pip, was standing next to him with her ears raised high, and she barked again when she saw Patch.

"Osbert!"

The old man's head bobbed up. He looked toward the sound of Patch's voice, trying to focus, and then saw who it was. He called out weakly, "You miserable cur! You little rotter! You . . ." But he interrupted himself with a wince of pain.

Patch dropped to his knees, panting. "Osbert, what happened? How long have you been here? Are you hurt?"

Osbert's face was pale and shining with perspiration. He shuffled his shoulders against the boulder to straighten himself. "Not sure—felt dizzy. Weak. Hurts in here." He touched his hand to his chest. "Help me up now, you villain. Got to get home." The words came in a whisper, as if even talking was painful.

Patch put a hand on his friend's shoulder. "Are you sure you can make it? Maybe you should stay here. We could make a fire, keep you warm all night."

Osbert shook his head and grasped Patch's wrist.

"Come on, take this old man home, before I knock you silly." He picked up the shepherd's crook that was lying next to him, and with the boy's help he got to his feet. Patch had an arm around Osbert's waist, Osbert an arm over Patch's shoulder. The old man wheezed and shuffled along, his right foot stronger than his left, which dragged feebly behind. After every few steps they stopped so Osbert could rest.

Patch heard a whimper behind them and looked back to see Pip lying on the ground, her ears flattened against her head. "Come on, Pip, he'll be all right," Patch said. The dog slunk forward, her belly practically scraping the ground.

At last Patch could hear the shushing sound of the river ahead. "We're getting near the Tumbles."

The sweat poured down Osbert's face, although the afternoon was growing cool. "I know," he said. "No choice, Patch. I'll never make it to the other bridge. We must cross here."

"We'll be fine," Patch said, squeezing the old man's side. As he and Osbert hobbled forward like an awkward four-legged beast, he peered at the shadows under the bridge. Across the river, to the west, the last sliver of sun dipped behind the trees, and the night began to draw its gloomy cloak across the world.

"Patch," Osbert said, almost too quietly to hear. "You know I never mean all those horrid things I say. You know that's just old Osbert playing the grumbler."

Patch grinned. "Oh shut your yap, you mangy bear. Let's get you home."

They stepped onto the bridge, watching the planks that creaked under their feet. Osbert was moving slower than ever now, wincing with every step.

When they were halfway across, Patch glanced behind him and saw that Pip had stopped on the other side. The dog was shaking, and her tail was curled down out of sight. She squatted and peed in the dirt.

Patch caught a whiff of something awful—a stench both rotten and sweet that made his stomach heave and the bile rise in his throat. Near the far side of the bridge, a hand—a monstrous, stone-colored, knobby-fingered hand—rose from the darkness below. It grasped and held the side, and a troll hauled itself up into the dying light. Osbert moaned and slumped to his knees, almost pulling Patch down with him.

"Run, Patchy," the old shepherd croaked.

Patch might have considered it, but a numbing fear had invaded his brain and legs, and he could only stare as the creature lurched to its feet, not three strides away. A troll, a living troll—he had never expected to see one, unless he dared one day to visit the Barren Gray, where such things usually roamed.

The troll came up, hunched with twisted shoulders. Had he stood straight, he might have been ten feet tall. His nose curled and sniffed. And then the hand rose and pointed a long, lumpy finger at them.

"I know your smell," the troll said, in a voice like a rusty saw rasping on wood. He swayed like a drunken man. "One of you has crossed my bridge before."

Patch blinked and gaped. He didn't know trolls could talk. He'd always thought of them as dumb, blundering beasts. But this one spoke—and *remembered* him.

The troll shuffled forward, and the broad finger that ended in a thick shovel-shaped nail stabbed again in their direction. "Yes, heard one of you on my bridge. Too fast for me, though. Jumps too high. But the other . . ."—he sniffed again, with a wet rattling sound deep in his nostrils—"too sick to run. Can't hardly walk now, can you?" And then the troll's wide mouth curled into a leer, as wide as a scythe.

Patch tried to help his old friend to his feet, but Osbert went limp in his arms. "You can't help me," Osbert said. "Run, Patch. For heaven's sake, run."

The troll took a half step forward, and then he paused and swayed. That was when Patch saw how diseased and decrepit this creature was. Red sores had erupted all over his pebbly, horned skin, which hung loose on his skeleton. Inside that crescent mouth, his black-red gums were populated by just a handful of jagged triangles, with black holes where other teeth had fallen out. The knee on one leg was grotesquely swollen, and the skin there was cracked and rotten. As Patch stared—he was seeing everything with slow dreamy clarity now—a maggot wriggled out from the cracks in the knee and plopped onto the bridge.

And something else, the most disturbing yet: those eyes. Eyes that were too small, grossly out of proportion with the rest of the ugly face. They were glazed all over, icy white, with a sickly yellow liquid streaming out like tears.

"Thought I'd had my last bite of flesh. Then I heard you two and thought, how about one more feast?" the troll rasped. "But then again, if you beg nicely, I may let you pass. What do you say?"

The troll kept his head turned to one side—listening for them instead of seeing, Patch realized. *Yes*, he thought, *you'd like to hear us answer. So you can find us. Because you're blind.*

The troll shuffled closer, moving sideways, and stretched out his lead arm. This creature might be nearing the end of his days, but he was still wider than any man Patch had seen. Those arms were still knotty with muscles and the fingers looked strong enough to crack a man's skull.

Patch bent to avoid the hand swiping over his head. Below him he saw Osbert slumped on the bridge, clutching his shepherd's crook, with his eyes shut against this horror and his mouth moving soundlessly. Patch pulled the long stick out of his friend's grasp. "Be still," he whispered.

The troll was right over them now, probing left and

right with his pointy fingers, sniffing deeply. Crouching, Patch reached out with the crook and tapped along the bridge beside the troll. It sounded like someone tiptoeing by.

The troll snarled and lurched in that direction, stepping near the bridge's edge. Patch stood up and swung the crook with all his might. There was a whoosh as the stick whipped through the air, and then a loud and sickening splat as it struck the back of the creature's swollen knee.

The troll howled. His knee crumpled, pinching the crook behind it and snapping off the curved end. The creature held his knee and teetered on the edge of the bridge, over the roiling waters. Patch drew back what was left of the staff, still five feet long. He raised it over his head and brought it down across the troll's back. The troll moaned and pitched forward, over the side and into the river. For a moment he disappeared, then came up sputtering, until the currents steered him near the bank, where the roots of the willows reached down to drink. The troll was swept under the curving roots and trapped beneath them, with the strength of the swollen river driving him under the surface. Patch saw the monster's head come up for a moment, fighting to rise above the foaming waters, and then it was gone. A moment later a gnarled foot bobbed up, moved not of its own accord but by the swirls and bubbles of the river.

People were shouting. Patch saw men and women running their way from the village, close enough to see what he'd just done. *They must have heard the troll scream,* he thought. He felt a touch at his ankle and saw Osbert smiling weakly up at him.

"Brave little tailor," the shepherd whispered hoarsely. "You killed a troll."

CHAPTER 2

"You know, Patch, anyone can sew a dress or a shirt for a person born with a pleasing shape," John the tailor said. "But it takes a real artist, a true master, to make the fat cow resemble the slender calf, or give an old buzzard the air of a handsome hawk. And you, my boy, you have the knack."

Patch smiled. He *was* doing well. Like his feet, his fingers were fast and nimble. He needed to be taught a thing only once, and every lesson was a gift he accepted eagerly and kept forever. He was not yet fourteen, but John already trusted him with more expensive materials, even the rare yards of brightly colored fabrics imported from distant lands.

The apprentice was working now at the bench next to his master. A month before, John had treated himself to a shiny new kit for sewing and repair work, and with a wide grin had presented Patch with his old set of tools (which weren't so old after all), along with the wooden coffer to hold it all. These were spread out before Patch as he worked: the needle case, the measuring tape, the shears, the piercing awl, a cube of beeswax, a dozen spools of colorful thread. There was a small pile of bone-white buttons as well, which Patch was sewing to a dress for a faithful customer, a wealthy and portly woman of the village.

John stood up to add another log to the fire blazing on the stone hearth in the center of the little shop. Sparks sputtered and winked out, and smoke curled up and out through the hole in the roof, while the occasional snowflake would drift in the same gap only to melt over the flames. "Here's a question for you, apprentice," he said over his shoulder. "How many bolts of cloth would we have needed to make a dress for that great troll of yours?"

"To make a funeral cloak, you mean. That decrepit thing came here to die. I just gave him a little push," said Patch.

"Ah, the modesty of our local hero," said John. He reached down to scratch Pip behind the ears and then held his hands palm out, close to the fire. Patch knew his master's fingers would start hurting after a few hours of sewing and that the cold weather made the pain worse. He was glad that his own skill was helping the tailor's business. It was gratifying to be useful.

And the help was needed, because business had been good since that spring day when the troll met its doom.

Especially as the story spread to surrounding towns, and people came to Crossfield to see the remains of the creature. An enterprising innkeeper named Bernard had dredged the troll's body out of the river, hacked it up, and boiled it in pieces in an enormous vat until only the bones were left—creating a fearsome stink that lingered for weeks. It was the bones that Bernard wanted. He built a gargantuan coffin in which he reassembled the skeleton. He kept the coffin in a back room of his tavern, along with cured samples of the troll's thick hide. Visitors paid to enter and gawk and—if Bernard wasn't watching—pocket a finger, tooth, or other small memento. This pilfering drove Bernard to the brink of madness. Now the innkeeper spent much of his time hovering over the remains, his thick eyebrows bunched in a scowl as he supervised the visitors to make sure no more pieces disappeared.

Of course, after they saw the bones, the next thing people wanted to see was the boy who had slain the beast. So they came down the street to the little tailor's shop. They would ask questions, and Patch would answer honestly. Everyone went away impressed with the tailor's apprentice, who insisted that it was not really such a heroic thing after all; in fact, he had been very lucky. But the visitors would think about that skeleton, stretched out nearly ten feet long, and they knew that this apprentice was simply being modest, as a good hero should be.

What was it about tailors, anyway? They would ask their friends when they retold the story. Because wasn't it just fifty years ago that another brave tailor had won his fame by killing a giant?

Patch snipped off the loose end of the thread on the last of the buttons and held the dress up for his master to inspect. "Have you ever seen better work?" he said.

But John had stepped away from the fire to peer out the window. "Hold on, Patch. Never seen these gents before. And look—that's the king's banner, ain't it? They came all that way in weather like this?"

The strangers were riding from the south in a horse-back procession, dark shapes on a snowy road. They wore heavy cloaks and hoods against the cold. The horses, steaming in the cold air, slowed as the party entered the village. The first rider carried the emblem of the king on a flag that hung from his lance. After him came a severe-looking man who pushed his hood back and surveyed the village. He had a narrow face with a hooked nose, and dark eyes that simmered under a heavy brow. His long hair and sharp beard were the color of rust. For a moment his glance lingered on the sign above the door of the tailor's shop.

After this man came a mounted servant, leading two horses with no riders. Then another servant, driving a light wagon pulled by a pair of horses. And finally, two more important-looking men, with swords by their sides.

People stepped out of their homes and shops to see

the visitors. The blacksmith bowed respectfully, and while his head was bent he secretly inspected the shoes of the horses, hoping there might be some business for him down there. The baker came out holding a tray with an assortment of his goods.

Patch heard John whistle in appreciation, and he knew that the tailor was admiring the fine clothing that was parading by. "Oh. That trim on the cape, very nice. Lined with fur, too—rabbit, I'll wager. And look at the tall one with the coppery hair, Patchy—that purple tunic you can see under his cloak? That's the king's shade of purple, no one else is supposed to wear it unless they're on his business. And all that gold piping and the gold belt— that's a lord, or some other nobleman for sure."

The potter's wife, Cordelia, was returning from the village well with a bucket of water in each hand. Never a shy one, she stopped to offer a cup to the tall lord with the dark eyes. Cordelia blushed as the man spoke to her—Patch could not hear what he said—and she responded by pointing down the road toward the inn.

"Maybe they'll stay at Bernard's for a few days," said John.

"If they can stand Bernard's company that long," Patch replied.

"Ha! Well said. You know, though, there might be some work for us in it. Wouldn't that be an honor? Never sewed anything for a genuine noble before."

As the party approached the inn, the door burst open

and Bernard rushed out to welcome them. Even at a distance, Patch and John could hear his flustered, booming voice.

"I most humbly and properly welcome you, my sirs ... sires . . . graces . . . uh, worships?" Bernard blathered, grinning up at the mounted men with a look of growing panic. He seized the tall lord's hand and pulled it toward his lips, trying to kiss the glove. "Please enter my domain and rest your weary ... er ... nobleness ...," he fumbled on. The glove slipped off the lord's resisting hand, and Bernard stared at it blankly. Then startling everyone, he bellowed over his shoulder, "Boy! Stable boy! Come get these bloody horses, you worthless toad!"

At last the entire party had dismounted and disappeared into the inn, practically shoved by Bernard, leaving the horses and the wagon to the hapless stable boy.

The tailor and his apprentice went back into the warmth of the shop, shaking their heads and chuckling. Patch tried to return to his work but found himself wandering to the window again and again to look down the road toward the inn.

"Master, do you suppose ..."

"Oh, go on, Patch, find out what's going on over there. And see if any of them needs a little tailoring while you're at it, eh? A torn sleeve, a frayed cuff, a missing button ..."

Patch got up to run, but John had one more thing to say. "Patch—just a bit of advice before you go. You might want to keep quiet. I know you, you're never shy about speaking up, but you haven't been around these noble types much. They like us common folk to know our place."

Patch grinned, tapped a finger against his lips, and dashed outside.

Seconds later he arrived at the inn. Even as he opened the door and stepped inside, he could hear Bernard's voice, unhappy and blustering. "But Lord Addison, you can't take them. I mean of course you *can*, a noble gent like yourself can do whatever he wants. But it simply isn't fair! A man has a right to his livelihood, don't he now?"

Patch stepped into a dark corner by the door, watching. Inside the inn, in the big room full of long tables where meals and ale were served, the tall man was speaking to Bernard.

"I would hope," Lord Addison said evenly, "that for the good of the kingdom you would gladly part with these bones. But whether you would part with them happily or unhappily is beside the point."

At these words Bernard's shoulders drooped and he hung his shaggy head.

"However," Addison said, producing a small pouch from his pocket, "a certain compensation might be appropriate, were you to have the remains loaded onto our cart by sunrise."

Bernard dropped to one knee and held his hands out to accept the pouch. "Thank you, your lordship!" He smiled crookedly at Addison through his bushy beard.

Patch noticed his fingers greedily working the pouch, trying to guess how many coins might be nestled inside. "I thank you kindly. It was my honor and duty to help rid the kingdom of this scourge."

Addison put one leg up to rest on a bench. "Indeed? Did you slay the creature? We were told by many people that a young tailor struck it down by himself, with only a shepherd's staff for a weapon."

Bernard's knees popped and crackled as he got to his feet. "Well, your lordship, Patch, that's the little tailor's name—an apprentice, actually, not a real tailor—he *was* on the bridge when the troll lost its balance and stumbled into the river. But it was me who hauled the troll out with a team of horses and hacked it to pieces before the beast could come back to its senses. Why, with one blow of my axe . . ."

Patch, standing in the shadows, gasped so loudly at this lie that one of Addison's men, a younger knight with a pleasant, handsome face, turned to see who was there. "Hello, boy. When did you sneak in?"

Bernard's eyes widened in a sudden flash of panic when he spotted Patch, and he began to babble. "Why here's the little apprentice now, my good sirs! Of course, when I said the troll lost its balance, I meant that Patch here *caused* it to lose its balance, because as you so wisely pointed out, he did strike the troll with a shepherd's crook—the blind troll, did I mention that the troll was blind? Fell right off the bridge, the sightless oaf. But in a way, I suppose Patch did—" Bernard stopped talking abruptly as Addison held up a gloved hand.

Another of Addison's knights, a burly man with a sprawling black beard, stepped forward for a closer look at Patch. "Him? This little pup killed the troll? Slew the beast in that box? I find that hard to believe."

"Well," Bernard said, piping up again, "it *was* a particularly old and feeble troll. And lame. Full of maggots, nearly dead . . ."

Patch was watching Addison carefully. His face hardly changed expression. But with the subtlest shifts—his eyes narrowing slightly, his nostrils dilating a fraction of an inch—he directed his gaze on Bernard in a way that made the innkeeper's jaw snap shut before another word could spill out. "Innkeeper, perhaps you should busy yourself preparing our rooms and our meals," Addison said quietly.

Bernard's ears turned red. "Of course, your lordship." He shuffled out of the room. The moment he passed through the doorway and disappeared, Patch could hear the sound of coins being emptied from the bag into Bernard's palm.

"And some ales while you're at it!" shouted the burly one after the innkeeper.

"Right!" Bernard called back, his voice cracking. There came the sound of coins hitting the floor, followed by muffled cursing.

Addison exhaled loudly, drew out a chair, and sat at

one of the tables. He pulled the gloves off his hands, finger by finger. "Young tailor, please tell me that you are not as talkative as that innkeeper."

"No, my lord," said Patch. "I mean yes. I mean I'm not."

"I'm glad. Now come over here and tell us: Did you really kill that troll?"

"I did, my lord. At least, I knocked him into the river, where he was trapped under the roots of a tree and drowned. Although I believe the troll would have died soon anyway. He was old and very sick."

Addison brushed his rusty beard with the back of his hand. "An honest answer. And is it true that there was an old man with you, a friend you were trying to save?"

"Yes, my lord," Patch said softly.

The younger of the knights sat down beside Patch. "That must have been quite an adventure, boy. Not everyone who confronts a troll is so lucky." A shadow crossed the young knight's face suddenly. He looked anxiously at Addison, as if he might have offended him somehow.

Addison's expression did not alter, and he waved his hand. "Never mind, Gosling."

The burly knight approached, holding something that might have been mistaken for a square of leather, but it was a couple of inches thick. Patch recognized it for what it was: a piece of hide that Bernard had taken from the drowned troll. "Have you seen this, Lord Addison?" he said, handing it to the rust-bearded nobleman.

Addison took the hide in his own hands, hefting it

and running his fingers across the pebbly outer surface.

"It's very tough," Patch said. "It took Bernard a long time to saw it off."

Addison offered Patch a frosty sideways glance. He passed the hide to Gosling, saying, "We should take this as well. It would be difficult for an arrow to pierce all the way through, wouldn't it?" Gosling nodded.

The door to the kitchen banged open, and Bernard returned bearing a tray with three mugs. He put these down on the table where Addison sat, then tucked the tray under his arm and stood there, rocking on the balls of his feet and glancing nervously toward the piece of troll hide.

"Something to eat, if you please," said Addison. "For us and the boy. Then you will kindly leave us be." Bernard looked down at Patch, offered a fleeting, fraudulent smile to Lord Addison and the knights, and then left the room again, muttering when he thought he was beyond earshot. Gosling laughed and leaned back in his chair. "What a charming fellow. Don't you think, Mannon?"

The burly knight snorted. "Northerners."

"Your name is Patch, is that correct?" asked Addison.

"Yes, my lord."

"I will get directly to the heart of the matter. My name is Lord Addison. My companions here are Gosling and Mannon." The two men nodded at their introductions, Gosling with a smile and Mannon with a grunt. "Word of your encounter with the troll has reached Dartham, and King Milo has taken a particular interest in your story. I have been sent to find you and bring you back to Dartham. There you will be introduced to the court and will tell them about your encounter with the monster."

Patch's mouth had slowly opened as Addison spoke. He stood there blinking. *Dartham, the castle on the river. Home of the king.* He'd dreamed of seeing it one day, but had never imagined he'd ever walk inside.

Addison said, "I trust you will not object. The king was adamant."

Gosling leaned forward, grinning. "Addison, I think you've stunned him. Shall I shake him until he recovers?"

Patch found his voice at last. "It's just so—I never expected—of course I don't object!"

"Very good. Not that it would have mattered. Like that pile of bones, you would have come either way," said Addison without emotion. "There is an important council in three days, and we must reach Dartham by then. Which means we leave in the morning."

CHAPTER 3

"**M**y apprentice, going to meet the king. And the young queen as well—I've heard she's a beauty! My mind can hardly absorb the idea! Here, Patch, take your tools, you might find some work along the way." John stuffed the coffer into a bag with the rest of Patch's belongings.

"You'll send word to my parents, won't you?"

"Of course. Patch, they will be so proud."

Patch knotted the cord at the top of the bag, but his eyes were on the tailor, warming his hands before the fire again. "Master, you're certain you'll be all right without me?"

"Sure, Patchy. The hands are fine, it's just this cold makes 'em stiff. But this winter has to end sometime, doesn't it?"

Somewhere not far away a rooster crowed, and as if that were his cue, Addison stepped into the tailor's shop. The nobleman was so tall he had to bend a little as he came through the door. "Are you ready to go, young apprentice?"

"Yes, my lord. I don't have much to bring. But there's one thing I'd like to do, if I can have a moment. . . ."

Addison tugged at the cuff of one glove. "If it won't take long."

"No, my lord," Patch said. He turned to the tailor. "I'm just going to run over to say good-bye to Osbert."

John's eyes crinkled, and he smiled. "Of course you are. Then come back and give me your farewell."

Patch dashed out, leaving Addison and the tailor behind in the little shop. John cleared his throat and said, "Pardon me, but I notice the end of your sleeve is frayed. Perhaps we can do something about that while you wait?"

Patch stood on the hill overlooking Crossfield, among the snow-covered gravestones. He had said good-bye to his friend, but Osbert of course did not answer.

Below him the town was waking. Still in the clutches of the longest winter in memory, it was a dormant place with just a few traces of activity: fragrant smoke curling from the baker's chimney, a steady clanging from the blacksmith's shop.

Outside Bernard's inn, Patch saw Addison's knights. Mannon, who seemed like a surly beast who would best be avoided, had thrown a rope over the high branch of a tree and was holding one end. At the other end, suspended a dozen feet above the ground, was a fat round sack. Gosling was standing several paces away with his bow and arrow ready. While Mannon pulled on the rope to keep the sack bobbing and swinging, Gosling fired arrows at the target. When the first one struck, the sack spun around, and Patch saw the ugly face that had been painted there. The practice ended suddenly when Addison strode out of the tailor's shop and began calling instructions. Mannon released the rope and gathered up the target, and Gosling ran to retrieve the arrows that had missed. The rest of the party from Dartham emerged from the inn and the stables. The wagon, with the troll bones already on board, rolled into view.

It was time to go. Patch hurried down the frozen hill, stepping in the same tracks he'd made on the way up to the cemetery.

Addison said they would ride all day to the town of Half, where they could eat and rest before the next day's journey to Dartham. Patch hadn't been on a horse for a long time, and it took an hour or two before he felt steady in the saddle. A bitter wind was blowing, sending flecks of ice into every gap in his clothing. Everyone in the party kept their heads down and their hoods drawn up against the cold.

Patch was stuck in the procession with the wagon and servants behind him and Mannon in front. "Will this winter never end?" Mannon growled. He shook his fist at the gray skies and went on muttering to himself.

Patch decided not to try to strike up a conversation with that ill-tempered knight, though his mind was full of questions.

In the afternoon the road widened, and Patch was glad to see Gosling spur his horse past the wagon to ride beside him. Gosling had a happy bearing about him and a face that seemed to naturally settle into a smile.

"Hello, Patch."

"Hello, Sir Gosling."

"Gosling will do," the young knight replied. "This must be exciting for you. Have you been to Dartham before?"

"I've never even been to Half before," Patch said.

"A grim and grimy little outpost. Big stone tower, wooden walls around the village. King keeps a small garrison there to maintain order in these parts. And speaking of the king, he must be eager to meet you, to send an important man like Addison all this way."

And Addison doesn't seem too happy about the chore, Patch thought. "Do you know, sir, what the king wants with me?"

Gosling grinned. "Well, let's just say that King Milo has a soft place in his heart for heroic peasants. You've heard of the Giant Killer, I presume? The Brave Little Tailor?"

"Yes, sir. Heard stories, anyway."

"Sure you have. Will Sweeting, that's his name. Slew a giant or two in his day. Though I imagine the stories have been, um, *embellished* after so many years. 'Seven at one blow,' all that stuff. Will was almost as young as you. Became a real hero to the common folk, and earned himself a handsome reward from Milo's father, who was the king back then. From what I hear, Milo grew up thinking that Will Sweeting was the cleverest, bravest man who ever lived." Gosling's horse suddenly jerked its head up and whinnied. The young knight bent down to whisper in its ear and pat its neck before turning back to Patch. "What was that all about? Anyway, all these years later, King Milo hears about this boy who knocked a troll off a bridge. And I suppose he thought, 'Well, the Brave Little Tailor might not be slaying giants anymore, but now we have the Brave Little Apprentice. The Troll Killer!'"

Mannon turned to glance back at them with a sour look. He pressed a finger against one side of his nose and blew, sending a giant gray gob flying from the other nostril. He kicked the side of his horse to put some distance between them.

"I don't think he likes me," Patch said.

"Ha! Only you and the rest of humanity," Gosling laughed. "Don't worry about Mannon, Patch. I know he acts like a brute, but he's truly a good fellow at heart, and the best friend I have. He's just angry over this errand the king sent us on."

"Oh." Patch looked back beyond the wagon, where Addison rode. "Is that why Lord Addison doesn't like me either—because he had to come all this way to get me?"

Gosling slapped Patch on the shoulder. "Don't take it

to heart, little tailor. Addison doesn't like or dislike any-one. He just does what he has to do, and does it better than anyone. He's a good man, Patch. Maybe the best the kingdom has. And he has his reasons for being grim, I suppose." Gosling scratched his horse's mane. He seemed to be deciding whether or not to continue. "He was never the most carefree fellow to begin with. But he lost his brother not too long ago. Hasn't been the same since."

"Oh." Patch took a deep breath. He and Gosling rode side by side in silence for an hour or more. The road entered a forest of pine that sheltered them from the bite and the roar of wind. The only sounds were the *clop-clop* of hooves and the creak of the wagon's wheels, until Mannon's horse reared up and stabbed the air with its front hooves. Mannon cursed it and pulled back on the reins until the horse calmed down.

When all was quiet again, Patch ventured, "How did Addison's brother die?"

Gosling smiled sadly. "A troll killed him, Patch."

"No . . ."

"Oh, yes. Giles Addison was a brave man. At the king's request, he went to explore the Barren Gray—where the trolls come from. He never came back. All they found was the horse's saddle and Giles's bloody armor. Torn open and squashed flat."

Patch glanced back at Addison again. The hood was drawn tight around the stern man's face. All you could see within the shadows were the red-brown beard and the straight, expressionless line of his mouth.

"Gosling, are you going to talk all the way to Half?" grumbled Mannon over his shoulder.

"It's possible, my dear friend," Gosling called back. "Since we're nearly there."

"Maybe there's a barber there to cut that hair of yours," Mannon snapped. "It's getting a little too long and lovely, don't you think? I could take you for a woman."

"Why, Patch," Gosling said. "I think Mannon just proposed to me!"

"Quiet!" Addison called out from behind, so suddenly that Patch had to stifle his giggle. The lord had thrown his hood back and was stretched high in his saddle. "Do you hear that?"

The procession came to a stop. At first Patch only heard the wind whistling across the tops of the trees. But then he could hear it too: a high voice calling from the forest and growing louder.

"My lords! Stay away, my lords!" A young man burst out of the evergreens and ran to them. His eyes were bulging and tears were streaming down his cheeks. "The v-village is in ruins! They attacked—stole our livestock, m-m-murdered the ones who fought! People f-f-fled, hiding in the woods!"

Addison dismounted and seized the man's shoulders. "Who, man? Who attacked you?"

The stranger's mouth was twisted with anguish, and they could just make out what he said. "T-t-trolls!"

Addison stared down the road in the direction of Half. Mannon scanned the woods, one eye squinting. Gosling looked at the stranger, while his hands went from the sword strapped to his horse to the quiver of arrows that was slung on his back.

"Did you say trolls? Was there more than one?" asked Addison. "Calm yourself, man, and answer me."

The man straightened up in Addison's grasp. He dragged his sleeve under his nose and sniffed. "More than one? M-more than a dozen!"

Mannon turned to Gosling. "So it's true."

"What is your name?" Addison asked the stranger.

"R-R-Roger," the stranger replied.

"Roger, when did this happen?"

"J-just today—this aftern-n-noon."

"Hold on," said Mannon. "Half is surrounded by a wall. How did the trolls get in?"

Roger moaned. "The wall? They tore the wall apart, that's how!"

"Are the trolls still there?" asked Addison.

"Not now—b-but what if they come back?"

"Come, we'll take you home," Addison said. "You may ride on the wagon."

Roger's eyes grew even wider. He stepped back, twisting out of Addison's grasp. "No! I won't go b-back! If you'd seen them, n-n-neither would you!" And he turned and charged back into the forest.

Addison watched him go, with an expression that never changed. "Well. Let us go without him, then," he said, and mounted his horse.

"Are you sure this is wise, Addison?" Gosling called.

"Where else can we go? It will be dark soon. We need to rest, and we can't camp out in this cold."

"But what if they *do* come back?" Mannon said.

"Yes," agreed Gosling. "And here we are with a box of troll bones—'Excuse me, Brother Troll, I think we have what's left of your uncle here.'"

"Why should we be afraid?" Addison said, jerking his head in Patch's direction. "The Troll Killer is with us." He spurred his horse and led the way down the road toward Half.

The horses grew more and more agitated the closer they got to the village. And when Half finally came into view, Patch realized what was frightening them: Down the wind came the faintest whiff of the rancid-sweet smell that he remembered from the troll on the bridge.

There was once a wall that completely surrounded the town, and a tall, strong gate that allowed visitors to enter. Now that gate had been torn away and hurled to the side, and much of the wall lay in ruins.

They rode through the wide gap into Half. The wagon could not get far—there was too much wreckage on the ground, scattered everywhere. Buildings were trampled flat and others had their roofs torn off. Some were burning.

In the middle of the street was a sight that Patch knew would live in his memory forever, although he saw it for only an instant before turning his head the other way. It was a dead man. His arms and legs stuck out from under the blanket that covered him at angles that didn't make sense to Patch's eye.

People were just emerging from their hiding places and beginning to sort through the ruined buildings. They called for their mothers, fathers, siblings, and friends.

"Do you see any of the garrison?" Addison asked.

"How many soldiers did the king have here?" Patch whispered to Gosling.

"At least twenty."

"Over there," Mannon said, gesturing. A young soldier was coming toward them, limping. He was young, like Gosling. He had a scabbard at his side, but no sword. His tunic was stained with the signs of battle.

"Lord Addison, I don't know if you remember me. Helias Swain. I trained under your sword a few years back," he said.

Addison nodded at him. "I do remember. What happened here?"

Swain bowed his head. "We knew they were out there. Someone had seen them, coming across the hills. We had archers waiting for them on top of the wall. We were excited—sure we could fight them off." He paused, shaking his head.

"Please go on, Master Swain."

"Three of them charged the gate. The others hurled stones at us from afar. Big stones—bigger than your head. It was like catapults, but worse—so much faster, so much more accurate. The first volley took three archers off the wall. Dead, just like that. And then the gate came crashing down, and they all charged in."

"How many?"

Swain put a hand over his eyes. "Don't know—it was madness, they were everywhere. Ten, maybe. No, more. Twelve? We kept fighting, but our arrows were like burrs in a bear's hide. They didn't trouble them at all."

Gosling dismounted. He put an arm across Swain's shoulder. "Where is the rest of the garrison now, friend?"

"Killed. Or still hiding. Some ran away." Swain wiped at one eye with the back of a gloved hand. "I don't understand—look what they did to the tower!"

Patch looked where Swain was pointing. If there had been a tower there once, it was nothing but a great heap of stones now.

Swain's voice grew unsteady. "We weren't fighting anymore. We'd given up. They'd taken our livestock. Then suddenly, two of them just set upon the tower— like they were pulling it down to amuse themselves. That tower's stood for a hundred years, and it took just two of them to bring it down!"

They all stood, staring at the rubble. "Didn't know they were that strong," Gosling said.

Nearby, a building that was leaning dangerously to one side collapsed entirely. Somewhere behind them an infant cried.

"Sorry we weren't here to help," Mannon said.

"Don't be sorry," Swain replied. "Be thankful."

CHAPTER 4

They rode out from Half early the next morning.

"A fine restful evening that was," Gosling said through a yawn. They had slept only a few hours in what was left of the soldiers' barracks. Deep into the night, Lord Addison and the knights and their servants had worked with the people of Half to keep the flames from consuming the rest of the town. Even as they left, some ruins smoldered still, and the smell of burnt embers haunted the air.

Patch felt thickheaded and drained. Only the chill in the air and his saddle-sore body kept him awake.

Just beyond Half, they crossed a bridge that spanned the Cald River. The Cald was wide and black and cluttered with broken slabs of gray ice, for it ran too swift to freeze over completely. The road along the east bank would take them to Dartham. "Before evening, if we make haste," Addison said.

They rode straight on for hours, until Addison reined

his horse in suddenly and held his hand up, signaling them all to stop.

"Finally," Mannon growled, "because I really have to p—"

"Quiet!" Addison snapped. He was looking at something across the river. Then Patch saw it too.

A troll was standing on the opposite riverbank, staring at them without moving. *Probably watching us since we trotted into view*, Patch thought, shivering. This one was bigger than the Crossfield troll, by a full head at least. And there was nothing skeletal or sickly about this beast. His brawny arms were as thick as the wooden barrel he was holding.

The creature was stone gray, and the primitive leather garment that covered him from shoulders to knees was the same color as his skin. They might have passed right by, mistaking him for a boulder jutting out of the snow, if Addison's eyes had not been so keen.

When the troll realized he'd been seen, he lowered his head and hissed at them.

"Greetings to you, too, Brother Troll!" Gosling shouted.

"What's he doing?" Patch asked.

"Getting water for the rest," Addison said. "They are feasting. Look behind him." He pointed to the stream of smoke rising above the treetops.

"Feasting on what?" Gosling wondered.

"The livestock of Half," Mannon grumbled. "And worse,

I'll wager." He turned to Patch. "Well, apprentice—care to do battle with this one? Or did you forget your shepherd's crook?"

"No, thanks," Patch said, feeling the redness blossom in his cheeks. He glanced at Gosling, who half smiled and rolled his eyes. But the smile abruptly left Gosling's face when he looked back across the river.

A second troll had stepped out of the forest. This was a hulking monster, larger and broader than the first, with a white hide like limestone or chalk. He had a large pack strapped to his back, and he held a wooden club studded with iron spikes.

"That's a twelve-footer," Gosling said.

"Fifteen," said Mannon.

A tapering, coal black tongue slid across the chalky troll's upper lip. His strange silver eyes glanced at the river, where broken slabs of ice drifted among the deep waters. *Looking for a way to cross*, Patch thought. He too looked up and down the river to reassure himself that no crossing was possible.

Addison turned his horse to face the creatures. "Can you understand me?" he shouted.

The chalky troll cocked his head for a long moment. Then he finally replied, in a deep, coarse voice that sounded like it was rumbling up from some bottomless pit, "Yes. But come across, so I can hear you better. And bring your horse."

Addison seemed startled by the reply. He looked at

Patch, who nodded. "The Crossfield troll could talk too, my lord," he said.

Addison called back to the troll. "I'm afraid the water is too deep and swift for my horse, so I will raise my voice instead. Is there a leader among you? I wish to speak with him."

The troll paused again before answering. "They all answer to me."

"What name shall I call you?"

"Hurgoth."

"Well then, Hurgoth. I must ask you: Why have you and your kin left the Barren Gray? Why have you attacked our town and killed our people?"

Hurgoth leered at them. "We were only defending ourselves—it was they who attacked us, when we simply stopped by to say hello." The troll's head turned toward the wagon. "Tell me, what is in that box?"

The fellow driving the cart glanced back at his cargo and shifted uncomfortably in his seat. Mannon cleared his throat loudly.

Addison replied evenly, "That is our business, not yours. You have entered the domain of King Milo. By his authority, I order you to return to your home."

Hurgoth stared for a while before spitting back his answer. "We don't recognize that authority! And as long as you're asking questions, ask your Milo why he sends his spies into our lands!"

Addison wavered in his saddle and he tightened his grip on the reins. Patch whispered to Gosling, "Is he talking about Lord Addison's brother—the one they killed?"

"I—I think so," Gosling said hoarsely.

Addison's voice was loud and stern. "Why are you here, Hurgoth? Declare your intentions!"

Hurgoth snickered. "Only to enjoy a fine meal. Come join us—we'd love to have you." He shouldered his club and walked into the forest, toward the rising smoke. The other monster dipped his barrel into the river, hissed a farewell, and disappeared in the trees as well.

The horses' hooves crunched in the thin crust of snow, and the wagon wheels groaned as they continued toward Dartham.

"You know, Mannon," Gosling remarked, "I once declared that you were the ugliest creature that ever walked the earth. Now I find I must apologize."

Mannon chuckled. "Yes, and I can imagine what you'll say when we battle these things: 'Not the face, Brother Troll, anything but my pretty face!'"

Just ahead was the first of many villages they would pass on the rest of the trip to Dartham. Word of the attack had spread quickly, and a group of villagers ran to them, calling out questions.

"Is it true about the trolls?"

"Are they coming this way?"

"What about our children?"

"Will the king protect us?"

Lord Addison held up one hand to quiet them. He told them what he knew of the attack on Half. "As for where they are now, or what they want, I am not certain. So do not panic, but be watchful. Keep your children close. Post sentries, particularly around your livestock. And if the trolls come, don't try to fight them. Just hide yourselves and send word to Dartham."

"And the dogs—watch your dogs," Patch called out. He was thinking of Osbert's dog, Pip, and how he'd behaved at the bridge that awful day.

"Dogs?" Addison asked, turning slowly toward Patch with one eyebrow raised.

Patch winced. *There you go again, running your mouth.* His voice squeaked as he replied: "Well—yes, my lord. I think the dogs might know the trolls are around before we do. They smell them . . . or something . . ." When Patch looked around and saw everyone staring at him, his voice trailed off. Behind his back, he heard Mannon snort.

Later, when they were back on the road, Mannon trotted up beside him. "You know, apprentice, if Lord Addison wanted you to wag your tongue, I'm sure he would have asked you. Dogs—ha!" He spurred his horse and moved ahead.

Patch didn't speak again for hours. He let himself fall back in line and rode behind the wagon with the servants, who kept their distance from him, perhaps to avoid earning a share of Mannon's foul temper.

Late that afternoon the river that had been their companion all this way poured into a wide lake covered in thick black ice. "Lake Deop," the wagon driver replied when Patch asked its name.

They passed by other villages and farms along the way and met other travelers. This slowed their journey, as Addison was obliged to offer the same advice and explanations to each group of anxious people.

At a town called Shorham, when the usual group swarmed around Addison, Patch guided his horse away to put some distance between himself and Mannon. He found a trough of water where the horse could drink and dismounted to stretch his aching legs. Not far down the road, he heard a sudden burst of laughter and saw a small crowd of women and children gathered in a circle, looking down at something. Patch walked over to see what was amusing them.

A man was lying there on the ground, and he had twisted himself into the strangest position. He was rocking on his back, and both of his ankles were tucked behind his neck. His long arms were wrapped around the knees, and his chin rested on his interlaced fingers, just above his own buttocks.

Patch broke into a grin, though the sight reminded him how much his own muscles ached from the hours on horseback. The women were staring with widened eyes and giggling behind their hands, and the children jumped and clapped.

"Now, my good folk," the contorted man said in an odd, high voice that quavered and cracked. "I need a bit of help. You, my good lady, would you lend a fool a hand?"

"Who, me?" said a plump woman in the crowd. The woman next to her pushed her forward, shouting, "Go on, Millicent, help the fool!"

"Yes, the lovely Millicent! Would you kindly give my nose a squeeze? I would do it myself, but I have tied this knot too tight. That's right, go ahead . . ."

"You're a strange one," Millicent said, chuckling. She approached cautiously, coming no closer than was necessary, then reached down toward the smiling face and squeezed the nose. And when she did, the fool unleashed an explosive, thunderous fart. Millicent yipped and fell back on her behind. The crowd gasped, and an instant later they roared with laughter. Patch couldn't help but laugh along with them, especially when the contorted man waved at the air before his nose with a ludicrous expression of mock disgust.

The crowd applauded, and the fool at last unfolded himself and stood up. He was tall and gangly, with thin arms and legs that moved as if there were no bones inside. His neck was exceptionally long, and his tongue lolled outside his open, happy mouth. His head was shaped like a gourd, round at the cheeks and narrow on top, where yellow hair jutted in every direction, like a haystack where children had played.

"Hoo ha!" he shouted. "Simon Oddfellow at your service, my good people!"

There was a sudden cry from outside the circle, and another strange man burst in. His head was as hairless as an egg, and he was dressed in a filthy quilt of multi-colored rags. He slapped at Simon with both hands, bellowing, "Get out, you! This is my town, my town! You're not wanted here!"

The crowd laughed anew, as if this, too, was an act, but Patch didn't laugh with them now. "Yeah, one fool's enough," said one of the older boys in the crowd, and he threw a stone at Simon. Other boys joined in, and Simon backed away. He threw his hands up around his face, shouted "Ooh! Ooh!" and ran back and forth to dodge the stones, and the roar of laughter grew.

Simon had been forced toward the lake, and he ran onto the ice. "Well! Maybe the folk are nicer on the other side," he shouted back. Patch watched him turn and walk—no, *skip*—across the vast flat surface. The opposite shore was miles away. The bald fellow made rude gestures after Simon and broke into a madcap dance on the shore, while the people of Shorham laughed and clapped.

"You—apprentice! We're leaving," a gruff voice called. Patch turned to see Mannon staring down at him. The smirk was visible through his beard.

"Perhaps you'll remember to tether your horse next time," Mannon said. Patch saw his horse, a hundred yards away, heading in the wrong direction. He ran to retrieve it, wishing he were a grown man, strong enough to knock Mannon right out of his saddle.

The sun had slipped out of sight by the time they reached the south end of the lake, where the river Cald was reborn. A mile later, as the stars flickered on overhead, the river came to a rise in the land and divided around it.

"Almost there," Gosling said, trotting up beside Patch again. "What do you know about Dartham Castle?"

"Nothing, really, sir. Except the king and queen live there."

"Well. Did you see the river split in two? It will reconcile, not two miles downstream. In the meantime, there's a space of land between the two, a lovely fertile diamond with a hill in the middle, and that's where Dartham sits. We're crossing to that river island now."

There was the clatter of hooves on wood ahead, and rolling wheels, and then Patch and Gosling followed the rest of the party across the bridge.

"You see, Patch, any army that tries to take Dartham has to take the bridges first, then trudge up the hill with arrows coming down like rain, before they even get to the walls. It's a mighty stronghold, Dartham."

They rode through fields and past barns and huts.

Inside were the people who cultivated the land for three seasons, and now spent this relentless winter huddled against the cold.

Gosling said, "Look now, Patch."

Before him, Patch saw an imposing black shape against a backdrop of stars: sprawling walls with towers rising at the corners, and watch-turrets sprouting even higher. Beyond the walls, Patch could see the keep, the great stone building inside the walls where the royals dwelled.

"See the jagged stonework at the top of the walls? It protects our defenders. We call those battlements," Gosling told Patch.

A horn sounded as they drew closer, and torches gathered along the top of the wall directly before them. They crossed a drawbridge over the ditch that surrounded the walls and arrived at a gatehouse in the outer wall. Men stood on the parapet above the gate, holding the torches. When the constable recognized Lord Addison, he shouted an order down the far side of the wall. Patch heard the screech and rattle of heavy iron chains, and a spiked ironclad grate that barred the doors began to rise. "We call that a portcullis," Gosling whispered to Patch.

The tall oaken doors, immensely thick, swung open. A small feline shape darted out and sprinted past the travelers, over the drawbridge. "And we call that a pussycat," Mannon jeered in a singsong voice.

Gosling chuckled. "A greater wit never lived, my portly friend. Patch, the winch room is just above this passage we're about to enter. The winches raise and lower the portcullises. You'll have to pop in to see it. Marvelous machinery."

As their horses trotted through the short passage under the gatehouse, Gosling tapped Patch on the shoulder and pointed up. In the ceiling of the passage, Patch saw small rectangular openings into the room above. Men were peering down at them. "More defenses. We can fire arrows down through those holes at anyone who gets this far," Gosling said.

At the far end of the passage, Patch saw the second, inner portcullis, already up, and he marveled at the strength of Dartham's fortifications. They passed into the courtyard, where stable boys bustled from the darkness to lead their horses away. Patch noticed Addison's head inclined upward, staring at something overhead. All the windows of Dartham were dark, except for a dim light at one balcony over the main door of the keep. A woman was there, looking down, a silhouette as slender and graceful as a black swan. Patch was so entranced that it startled him when a pale, thin man suddenly appeared in front of them, dressed in long robes and holding a staff of polished white wood in one hand and a candlestick in the other.

"Greetings, Lord Addison," he said. "It is good to see you again."

"And you, too, Basilus, old friend."

Basilus lowered his head and closed his eyes. "It was my honor to serve your brother. I grieve for his loss."

A gentle cough came from Addison's throat. "Thank you, Basilus. I know Giles valued your service. May you serve the king as well as you served him."

Basilus bowed. "As for the king, my lord, he asked to see you, no matter what time you arrived tonight."

"Very well," Addison said, before turning to the others. "I'm sure the rest of you are anxious to put this day behind us. So good night, gentlemen. And Patch. Until we convene in the morning."

Addison went into the keep with Basilus. "This way to the barracks," Gosling said, and they turned toward a separate building, long and low and made of timbers. Inside, where it smelled of smoke and straw and sweat, a score of mattresses surrounded a smoldering fire. Under heaps of wool and fur slept an unknown number of men. Gosling and Mannon kicked off their boots and burrowed in among them.

Patch found an unoccupied spot next to a snoring stranger. He closed his eyes and a jumble of images drifted across his mind—stern Addison, vile Hurgoth, mocking Mannon, ridiculous Simon, a lovely figure in black—before he swiftly plummeted into dreamless sleep.

Addison"

CHAPTER 5

Patch was the last to wake up. He stumbled out of the
barracks into yet another cold winter morning. The light
of the sun had transformed the landscape.

The courtyard was far bigger than he had imagined—
all of Crossfield could have fit inside, and more. He'd
expected open ground, but it was filled with structures
of all sizes. There was a chapel, the largest building after
the keep. There were storehouses and stables, a well
house and thatch-roofed workshops for coopers, candle
makers, potters, and more. Nearby a smith worked at a
forge, sparks flying as he hammered on a smoldering bar
of iron. In a far corner was a vineyard, just naked sticks
lashed to wooden frames in this frigid season. There was
a small pond close to where Patch stood. Through a hole
that had been chopped through the foot-thick ice, he
could see eels and fish swimming about.

"There you are." It was Addison, stepping out from

the keep's main door. "We are about to begin. If you are quite ready."

Patch followed him to the tall doors, where Addison turned, blocking the threshold. "May I offer you some advice?"

"Of course, my lord," Patch replied.

"We are here to discuss grave matters. At this meeting there will be scholars, knights, and noble folk. If I were you, I would understand my place. I would answer questions that were asked of me, of course. Other than that, I would remain silent, and let the leaders of this kingdom decide what they will."

Patch felt his cheeks flush red. Addison stared down, expressionless. "Of course, young apprentice, this is only my advice. You can choose to ignore it. But it seems to me that a peasant like yourself, in the company of the king . . ."

"I understand," Patch said while Addison paused. "Thank you, Lord Addison." He slowed to let the nobleman walk ahead of him.

Patch's eyes widened as he entered the great hall of Dartham. Before this moment, Bernard's tavern held the largest room he'd ever seen, and this one had to be twenty times the size. The ceiling seemed as high as the heavens, and it was made of heavy beams and planks that served as the floor for the rooms above. Towering tapestries hung on the walls, flanking arched openings that led to other areas of the keep. An enormous wooden table stood in the center, littered with maps and parchments and leather-bound books. There was room for twenty people or more in the chairs that lined three of its sides. Half were occupied already, while enough men to fill the rest stood talking. As Addison walked in, many of them nodded his way.

Patch saw Bernard's box next to the table, along with other containers. He felt a surge of pride when he saw some men clustered around the box, looking at the remains of *his* troll, the one he'd knocked off the bridge. One of the knights held up the square of troll hide for the others to see, and the rest marveled over the tough skin, more than two inches thick.

Against one wall was a cavernous fireplace with a roaring blaze that bathed the room in a warm orange light and cast quivering shadows onto the stone walls. Near the fire, apart from everyone else, Patch saw a thin, bent old man with a long white beard, slouched in a comfortable chair and covered with blankets despite being so close to the flames. Patch thought at first that he was sleeping, but the old man's eyes were open. What he was looking at Patch could not guess—the elder's eyes seemed to focus on a distant point that was far beyond even these walls. The old man's mouth moved soundlessly, and he rocked gently as he sat.

Suddenly, a voice boomed out behind Patch. "Is that the apprentice? Is that him, Addison?" The voice belonged to a round man with a head of thick, curly hair that merged with an equally dense beard, so that it gave the impression of an auburn wreath circling his moon-like face. He had sparkling eyes and a mouth that seemed accustomed to smiling, and he bustled toward them with outstretched hands.

"It is, Your Majesty," Addison said, bowing slightly.

As the round man drew close, Patch noticed the fine purple garments trimmed with gold, and the modest crown almost lost in that unruly hair. *King Milo.* Panic flooded Patch's brain. Not knowing exactly what to do, he dropped abruptly to his knees and lowered his head. "It is an honor to meet you, Your Majesty." The gesture was clumsy, and he heard some chuckles from the men in the room.

"Oh, get up, get up," said Milo. He clutched the material at Patch's shoulder and hauled him to his feet. "We are so pleased to meet you. You're a hero, son. An inspiration to all the common folk. I hope you're ready to tell us all about your battle with the troll. We have much to learn today." He lifted his head to search the room. "Are we ready to begin? Where is Griswold? Where is our scholar?"

"Here, Your Majesty," a wheezy voice answered. A grizzled-looking man in a long gray robe hobbled into the room, struggling to control the bundles of scrolls and books he held under each arm. Griswold walked to the side of the table without chairs and dropped his burden there with the rest of his materials. He talked quietly to himself as he arranged them. "Now where is the—oh yes, there it is. Did I bring . . . of course, it's right here, I'm losing my mind. But where—don't tell me I—confound it, that's not it. . . ."

Milo's cheerful laugh rang out. "Come, my friends, take your places around the table. Perhaps by then Griswold will be ready." The men moved quickly to their seats. Milo took the centermost chair, with a back that towered above the rest. Addison sat on the king's right side, and Mannon and Gosling took the next places. Gosling waved Patch over to sit beside him. Patch's stomach was rumbling, so he was thrilled to see platters of salt fish and rye bread within reach. "Eat up, young tailor," Gosling whispered. "This could be a long meeting."

That sounded fine to Patch. He was fascinated by the scrolls and parchments, and delighted by this jovial king. During his journey with Addison and company, he'd formed the impression that the higher a noble ranked, the less friendly he became. But Milo contradicted that theory. Here was a grown man with the enthusiasm and warmth of a child.

Basilus, the king's steward, appeared next to the scholar with a goblet on a silver platter. "Wine for the king's honored guest?"

Griswold squinted at the offering. "No, wine has a terrible effect on me, dear Basilus. But I would ask for water if I might." He turned to face the king. "I am ready, Your Majesty." The king nodded his approval.

Griswold had spread out the map of the kingdom and its surrounding countries, an enormous book, a bundle of moldy scrolls, and sheets of parchment that looked ready to disintegrate in a strong breeze: the accumulated knowledge of the trolls. The old scholar watched with a satisfied smile as the king's men leaned closer to the table, taking care not to block the monarch's view. He took a few extra moments to arrange the items just so, and Patch could tell that he was enjoying this moment. Men of the sword and the arrow were so often the heroes, Patch thought, but now Griswold had been summoned from wherever he lived, and all these powerful knights and lords were itching to hear what the learned man had to say.

He straightened up, cleared his throat, and rubbed his hands together. "Shall I begin with a poem? Perhaps you know it already:

> *Keen of smell*
> *Dull of sight*
> *In the cold*
> *They stalk the night.*
> *Eyes so small*
> *Mouth so wide*
> *Sharp the tooth*
> *And thick the hide.*
> *Nails like spades*
> *To dig their holes.*

Keep thou safe
From wicked trolls.
No warmth
No sun
No friends
No one
Can keep thou safe
From wicked trolls."

There were a few smiles around the table, a nod or two of recognition, and some impatient glances. Griswold shrugged. "Learned that when I was just a child myself. It's not entirely accurate. But then, it's only a poem meant to keep the children from wandering too far from home." He turned the map around so that it faced the king. "Well, sire. As you know, the stone trolls, or weeping trolls, as they are sometimes called— because of the noxious yellow stuff that always oozes from their eyes—are solitary creatures, living alone in their caves and skulking out to cause no end of evil. As far as we know they come from the Barren Gray, a mountainous area not visited by sensible men. The Gray is known for its desolation, its long winter, its rocky terrain, its lack of vegetation, and of course the trolls themselves. It is thought that the monsters feed mostly upon wild goats and pigs, except, of course, for the unlucky people whom they waylay.

"The trolls have rarely ventured far from that homeland. They are bolder in the winter than any other season. And the rare troll that wanders down during the summer prefers to stalk at night. Interestingly, only the male trolls are known to roam. Legend has it that somewhere deep in the Barren Gray is the Cradle of Trolls, a cavern where the she-trolls remain, caring for their broods.

"When the males leave the Gray, they most often follow the stony ridges that reach down into our kingdom like fingers."

Chairs creaked as the men leaned forward to consider the map. Griswold put his finger on the exquisite chart and traced a prominent ridge. "As you see here, one of the largest of these ridges runs southward, near the village of Crossfield. Now, Crossfield is not a significant place. I only mention it because we have rumors of a boy, a tailor's apprentice, who slew a troll here, and—oh!" Griswold's eyes had been moving from person to person around the table, and now settled on Patch.

"Good heavens, are you that boy? How nice to meet you! So it's true, then? Tell me, could your troll speak? He could? How interesting! I look forward to your story." Griswold looked up to address the entire gathering again. "At any rate, the appearance of a troll in a place such as Crossfield is typical. This lone troll simply followed the stony ridge until he found a convenient hole to live in.

"Now remember what I have told you as we follow the largest ridge. This one ranges farther south, yet still ends here, at least ten miles north of the town of Half."

Some of the men began to shift in their seats, as if suddenly uncomfortable. Milo stared intently at the scholar. "Yes," Griswold said. "Strange things are happening that, in all our learning, we have not witnessed before. First, the trolls are traveling together and even cooperating. Second, they have ventured many miles from the stony ground that they prefer.

"There is ample evidence that trolls are not comfortable for long away from such terrain. In fact, the historian Umber writes of one encounter where a troll emerged from its hole to chase a girl. He pursued her until she ran into a sunny meadow. Then he suddenly dashed off in the opposite direction, as if terrified. Incidents such as these have led some to believe that trolls are harmed by bright sunshine. And yet they have also been seen under the sun on mountainsides.

"These are powerful creatures, quick to anger and nearly impervious to attack. There is record of one troll being surrounded by a group of archers who emptied their quivers and put no less than fifty arrows in the beast, including three in the head. The troll plucked a tree out of the ground and began swatting the archers like flies.

"The use of fire is not recommended. It drives them into a murderous rage. Certainly it causes them pain, but it does not kill. Umber's chronicles tell us of one troll that was preying on a village. The men of the village threw buckets of oil on the beast and set him aflame. It is written that the troll's roar was heard from miles away. The troll tore the entire village apart.

"And yet, though they seem invulnerable to our attack, there are also instances of trolls simply dropping dead for reasons that are not understood. One spring about twenty years ago, a troll that was secretly observed suddenly went berserk, running in circles and slapping at his head. Then he simply fell to the ground, dead as a stone."

Milo sat, pursing his lips. He seemed about to speak when the doors to the hall opened and another knight came in, pulling off his gloves as he hurried across the floor.

"Ludowick," Milo called, with a hint of discontent in his tone. "I wondered where you had been."

"Forgive me, Your Highness," Ludowick said, bowing and then slumping into the sole remaining chair. "I was detained—you see, something has happened. The trolls again."

"Now what?" Mannon turned to Gosling and griped.

"I am afraid," Ludowick said to Milo, "that one of your wagons was intercepted. With many casks of your wine."

"Surely you're not so downcast over a few gallons of wine," Milo said. Then, looking closer at Ludowick's ashen face, he asked, "What is it, Ludowick?"

"Constancius was on the wagon, sire. He was proud of the wine. He wanted to deliver it personally."

"Constancius," Milo repeated quietly. "A good, good man. Ludowick, you must tell us what happened."

Basilus the steward appeared at Ludowick's shoulder and with great care placed a goblet in front of him. Ludowick paused for a moment, staring mournfully at the wine. Then he raised the goblet high. "First, a toast. To Constancius. Winemaker to the king."

"To Constancius," voices echoed around the table, and goblets clashed.

Ludowick wiped a sleeve across his mouth. "I was on my way here along the western road when I caught up with old Constancius, driving the wagon himself with a dozen casks or more. I rode beside him awhile, while he went on about his grapes and what this awful winter will do to next year's vintage. Finally, just when we were passing Lake Deop, I realized I was going to be late to Dartham, so I said good-bye and hurried ahead. But before I got far, I heard a fearsome noise behind me—horses screaming, and some grunts and howls that sent shivers down my spine. I turned around and went back—against my horse's better instincts, I must say—and there were trolls, ten or more, swarming the wagon. I won't tell you about Constancius or the horses. Perhaps if I never speak of what I saw, it will not forever haunt my dreams. The filthy beasts just ate, and laughed, and cracked open every cask and guzzled down every drop of your wine, my king." Ludowick bowed his head. "Sire, I am so sorry I was unable to prevent this from happening. I beg your forgiveness."

"You don't need to be forgiven, Ludowick. There

was nothing you could do," Milo replied.

"There was one thing I could do, sire," Ludowick said, lifting his head. There was fire in his eyes. "I tied my horse to a tree and followed the devils. I know where they live. In a hole in a hillside, not far from where the road passes Lake Deop."

"I know that place!" Basilus exclaimed. The knights turned to look at the steward. "I beg your pardon, sire," he said, staring at the floor. "But I grew up on the shore of the lake. That hole leads into a cavern, which is quite large. Even twenty trolls could live there."

"Yes," Ludowick said. "I got as close as I dared and spied on them for a while, to learn what I could. But soon two of them came out, sniffing the air and looking about. I cursed my carelessness—the wind was at my back, carrying my scent toward the trolls. They began to creep toward me, searching. I could either stay in hiding, or run and show myself before they got too close. I chose to flee. I could hear their steps thumping behind me, and every time I dared to turn around, they were getting closer. I ran for my horse—but I had doomed the poor beast to an awful death when I tied him to that tree, for another troll was there feasting on him. And when that troll saw me, he too began to chase me."

"Good heavens, man! How did you escape?" Milo cried.

"The lake, sire. I ran through the trees, past a little fisherman's house, and out onto the ice. The trolls would not follow me there. Too bad they did not, because Lake

Deop is well named—it drops off to a great depth only a few steps from shore, and the devils might have broken through the ice and drowned. But they stayed on the shore by that house, laughing and taunting and waving at me to come back. I cursed them and walked to Dartham, arriving just now with this unhappy story."

When Ludowick finished, Patch heard the men around the table inhaling deeply. Like him, many had forgotten to breathe as Ludowick told his tale.

Mannon growled and slammed his fist on the table. "Is there anything we can do to such creatures? They kill our people, feast on our livestock, tear our villages apart. We can't burn them. We can't pierce them with arrows. How do we fight them?"

"Could we roll stones into the opening of that cave and trap them inside?" Gosling offered.

Griswold shook his head. "They are cave dwellers, great diggers and tunnelers. They would be out in a moment."

"Our catapults—could they launch something large enough to crush them?" someone asked.

"You presume the trolls will stand still for us to target them. And even if we hit one, that would leave ten or more to slay," said Addison.

"This is a plight," the king said, shaking his head. "One troll wandering down to hunt is a dangerous pest. But a dozen, banded together—how can we deny such a force? Is there no weakness, Griswold?"

"They are not very clever. And their eyesight is said to

be weak, my king. But apart from that . . . ," Griswold replied, shrugging.

The king turned to look at the old white-bearded man sitting by the fire. "If only our friend was having one of his moments of clarity. He would have an idea for us, the clever one." Milo called out, "Can you hear me, Will? Are you listening?" But the old man did not stir.

Patch suddenly understood who it was in that chair by the fire: Will Sweeting, the Giant Killer. The Brave Little Tailor. A commoner like himself, a tailor even, who had risen up to become the greatest hero the kingdom had known. *And look at you now*, Patch thought sadly, *so frail and gray*. He barely heard the next thing the king said, or even realized that it was directed at him.

"But wait—I have almost forgotten. One among us has killed a troll. Perhaps he knows a way to slay a dozen. What do you say, young Patch?"

Every head turned Patch's way. In truth, an idea had been taking shape inside his mind while listening to Griswold. He hadn't thought it through or considered its drawbacks. But the king was asking for his opinion— why not offer it? As he started to speak, he saw Addison's eyes darken and narrow.

"Well, Your Majesty. I wondered—that is, I thought— we might poison them."

"Poison?" Mannon snorted. "And how do you plan to get them to take it?"

"What good would it do to poison one or two of

them?" someone at the far end of the table said.

"We would poison them all," said Patch.

"Ridiculous," said another knight, while others murmured.

"Quiet, all of you," said the king. "Young tailor, how could we poison them all?"

"That's what I'd like to know," Mannon grumbled under his breath.

Patch looked around at the staring faces. Even the steward was hovering close, listening curiously. Addison raised one eyebrow, as if to say, *I warned you not to speak.*

Patch cleared his throat, which had gone dry. "Well, I was thinking about how the trolls attacked the wagon with the king's wine. And how they all broke open the casks and drank it on the spot. We could send another wagon down the same road. But this time, the wine would be poisoned."

The men around the table looked at one another and turned to see how the king would respond. Milo leaned back slowly in his chair and scratched at his temple with one finger. Ludowick nodded and gently rapped the table with the knuckles of one fist. Addison had a distant look in his eyes.

"What if poison doesn't work on trolls?" asked Mannon.

Ludowick responded before Patch could speak. "Then the devils will never be the wiser."

"Fine, but what if it just makes them sick?"

"If they were all sick at once, they might be vulnerable to an attack," Ludowick said, his voice quickening.

"Yes," the king said. "Yes."

There was a long moment of silence, until Gosling spoke.

"It's not a *noble* plan, is it?"

"It's a nasty trick," agreed Mannon. "Should we stoop so low?"

Milo stood up slowly, pushing against the plush arms of his chair. He looked left and right, meeting the eye of everyone at the table. "Gentlemen. Stay in your seats, all of you. Allow me a moment alone to consider this." The king clasped his hands behind his back and walked, with his head bowed, around the curtain that was hung behind the great table.

The knights muttered quietly to one another. Gosling leaned close to Patch and whispered. "Seen this before. Takes a walk to clear his thoughts when there is a great decision to ponder. He'll have his mind made up in a moment."

Sure enough, Milo emerged a few minutes later. He stood in front of his chair, made fists of his hands, and pressed them against the tabletop.

"Desperate days call for dark deeds," the king said at last. The troll skull had been set on the table before him; he reached out and spun it to look into the face, all gaping eye sockets and thorny teeth. "I would never consider this way against a human enemy. But we poison mad dogs and rats, don't we? If we can find or brew the quantity of poison this plan requires, we will try it."

"I'll gladly drive that wagon," said Ludowick.

"Then I have a bit of advice for you, Ludowick," Griswold said. "Take a dog with you. Dogs make excellent sentries; they sniff out the presence of trolls before we can."

Patch tried to smile at Mannon, but the knight simply glared at the ceiling. He looked to Addison instead, and when he saw the cold stare that the nobleman had fixed on him, he shrank down in his seat.

When the meeting ended, the knights walked out of the great hall, discussing what they had heard. Patch stayed alone at the table, admiring the arching space over his head, so high he wouldn't have been surprised to see clouds drifting along.

"Clues," said a weak, rasping voice behind him. Patch turned. Will Sweeting, still sitting in his chair by the fire, was looking at him with clear, sharp eyes.

"What—what do you mean, sir?" Patch said, walking over to him.

The ancient man held out a trembling hand, and Patch took it. It was colder than it ought to have been, so near to the fire. "I heard clues," Sweeting said.

"You *were* listening!" Patch said. "But I don't understand. . . ."

Sweeting brought Patch's hand close to his face. "Good hands, nimble fingers," he said hoarsely, laboring to bring forth every word. "But nimble minds are needed more. Remember what Griswold said. Don't ask why they're here . . . ask why they never came before. What kept them away?"

Patch looked back where Griswold had stood. Sweeting was right. Just before Ludowick arrived with his sorry tale, Patch had been getting the feeling that there was a riddle to be solved.

"I think you're right. I feel it too. But what were the clues?" he asked.

The sound of rustling fabric caught his attention. There was a curtain behind the table, and the figure of a woman emerged from behind it. She was lovely, small and slender, with a river of glistening black hair that flowed down her back. She looked at Patch from the corner of her eye and smiled. A moment later she slipped through an archway. Patch did not doubt that this was the woman he'd seen on the balcony the night before; was it the queen?

When he looked back at Will Sweeting, the old man had slipped away again, staring at nothing and rocking gently in his chair. He did not respond when Patch called his name or took his hand.

Patch walked around the curtain behind the great table. There was a simple chair there, unoccupied. He went to it and put his hand on the wooden seat, feeling the warmth under his palm. A person could have sat there unseen, during this or any other council, and heard every word.

CHAPTER 6

$\mathcal{T}$here *was* enough poison. Indeed, many eyebrows were raised and glances exchanged when the multitude of toxins was brought before the king and his court the next morning. There was aconite, belladonna, thornapple, henbane, hemlock, bittersweet, arsenic, and mercury. There were lethal extracts from laurel berries, mushrooms, tares seeds, bitter almonds, and the pits of apricots and cherries. The physicians and apothecaries hastened to explain that these were used (in only the smallest quantities, of course) for the valid treatment of various maladies, for the control of insects, the disposal of mad animals, and other perfectly legitimate practices.

"Make certain the effect of the poison is delayed," Milo commanded, "so all the trolls may drink before any fall sick."

The physicians and apothecaries huddled together. After a loud and vigorous debate, they agreed on a formula and mixed the poisons into the wine. "Perhaps the strongest, deadliest potion ever brewed," one white-haired physician said when the work was done, wiping his hands over and over with a damp cloth.

Within an hour the twelve casks were loaded on the wagon, and Ludowick climbed aboard to drive it. Patch and the others followed on foot, staying out of sight in the forest by the road. They had left their horses farther back, with a group of soldiers who waited, spears and axes in hand. If the poison only sickened the trolls, Mannon would signal the fighters with the hunter's horn that was slung across his shoulder, and they would come to help finish the task.

"Ludowick's putting his neck on the line for this plan of yours, tailor boy," Mannon grumbled. Patch wanted to tell him, tell everyone, that it wasn't a plan at all. It was only something that had occurred to him just before Milo asked for his thoughts, and he wasn't sure in the least that it was a good idea. But things were in motion now, and he thought it would be better not to respond. Nothing he said would please Mannon, anyway.

"Don't worry, Mannon," said Gosling. "Ludowick's got a dog with him. He'll have plenty of warning if the trolls are near." He winked at Patch.

"The trolls' cavern is just up that hill," Addison said, gesturing at the opposite side of the road. "And this is where the winemaker was attacked." Patch looked to his right and saw the place that Ludowick had run to escape the trolls the day before. Past a scattering of evergreen trees, there was a wide flat beach where a tiny fisher-man's house stood. A boat was pulled on shore and turned upside down, waiting for warmer days when it might be useful again. Just beyond that sprawled the snow-swept ice of Lake Deop.

It was only a moment later that the hound at Ludowick's side leaped out of the wagon and ran, whin-ing, into the forest. Ludowick pulled back on the reins and the single ox that was hauling the wagon slowed and stopped. Ludowick stood up, peering at the hillside.

"Get out of there," Mannon whispered. As if hearing him, Ludowick vaulted over the side of the wagon and dashed into the forest. "Over here," Addison called, just loud enough to be heard, and Ludowick joined them, finding his own tree to hide behind. "They're coming," Ludowick said. It was another cold day, but Patch noticed sweat trickling down the knight's temples.

Patch saw shapes moving through the trees on the hillside, dark against the thin crust of frozen snow that remained on the ground. A group of the trolls stalked onto the road. Hurgoth, the massive troll they'd encoun-tered at the river, was among them—easy to spot with his pale, chalky skin and the small pack strapped to his back. He strode toward the ox, his spiked club in his hand. Patch closed his eyes as the club rose.

"Wait—what about the ox?" he'd said an hour before, when he realized his plan meant doom for the animal that hauled the poisoned wine. "There must be sacrifices,"

Addison had replied. "Or hadn't you considered that?"

The sound came, a terrible crack of wood on bone. When Patch looked up again, Hurgoth had picked up the ox in one hand—*one hand!*—and tossed it to another troll.

"Go on, fellows, have some wine," Gosling urged.

The trolls surrounded the wagon and laughed, pleased with their prize. A particularly fat troll lifted one of the casks and began to pry at the spigot. Hurgoth snarled at the troll, then turned to say something to the rest. The trolls lifted the dozen casks out of the wagon and carried them back up the hill.

"Didn't they drink the wine on the spot yesterday?" Addison said to Ludowick. Ludowick nodded, frowning.

"Maybe they're saving it to wash down the ox," said Gosling.

Addison stared up the hill at the retreating trolls. "Then we shall have to follow them."

Addison led the way to a ridge that overlooked the lair of the trolls. They lay on their stomachs and crawled to the edge to peer over. Below them, in a bowl-shaped depression in the hill, they could see the trolls milling around the gaping black mouth of their cave. The ox had been skewered and was suspended over a fire, and the casks of wine were in a pile, unopened.

"What do you suppose they're doing?" Mannon wondered, scratching the back of his neck.

"And where's Hurgoth?" Gosling asked.

As if to answer the question, Hurgoth emerged from the cave, trailing a rope behind him. He tugged at the rope, and a man came stumbling behind, with the other end of the rope knotted around his waist. The man was gangly and loose-limbed, with unkempt, straw-colored hair and—strangely—a loopy, happy grin.

When Patch saw him, his mouth dropped open, and he gulped in a lungful of ice-cold air.

"I've seen that fellow before," Mannon muttered, pointing.

"It's Simon," Patch groaned. "The fool from Shorham." He remembered Simon skipping off across the lake in search of a friendlier audience—unwittingly heading for the western shore, near this very place.

"What on earth are they doing with him?" said Ludowick.

Simon waved his hands at the trolls that surrounded him. "Hullo, boys!"

Hurgoth dropped something into the snow in front of the fool. Simon picked it up. It was a goblet.

"No . . . ," Patch moaned. He looked at the others. They were watching the trolls with bewildered expressions, except for Addison, who stared gravely back at Patch.

Hurgoth gestured toward the casks of wine. Simon looked at the casks, at Hurgoth, at the goblet in his hand, back at Hurgoth, and back at the casks again. Then his grin broadened into an enormous, open-mouthed smile. He shouted, "Hoo ha!" and pranced over to the casks.

"I don't believe this," Gosling said.

Patch felt a sickness in his stomach, a tightness in his throat. "They're making him drink the wine—making him taste it before they do?"

Ludowick said, "Remember—the poison's effects are delayed. It will not matter if the fool drinks first."

"Patch," Addison said. Patch turned to look into those dark, flinty eyes. Addison didn't have to speak—Patch understood the message. *There must be sacrifices.*

Patch shook his head. "But my lord . . . this . . . this isn't like the ox. This is a *person!*"

Below them, Simon stood in front of the casks. He held the goblet high and rubbed his belly in a broad circle, nodding gaily. The trolls gathered around him.

"He's just a fool," Mannon said. "Leading a wretched life."

"This is our chance to kill the trolls, Patch," Addison said. "You saw what they did at Half—what they're capable of. The life of one fool is not too high a price to pay. We may save hundreds more." He edged closer to Patch as he spoke. Now he was nearly arm's reach away.

Simon opened a spigot and bloodred wine gushed out, splashing over the edges of the goblet and staining the snow. His tongue hung out of his mouth, and he panted like a dog. He filled the goblet to the brim before closing the spigot. The trolls drew closer, forming a thick, high wall of pebbly flesh.

Patch could feel Addison's will pressing against him,

like a lion's paw on a mouse. He watched Simon raise the goblet toward the trolls, toasting them, and then bring it to his lips.

Suddenly it seemed to Patch that he'd stepped outside of his own mind somehow—because surely that couldn't be his own self leaping up and screaming, "Don't drink, Simon, it's poison!" And surely Addison wouldn't seize him by the collar and shake him and call him that awful word, and Gosling and Ludowick wouldn't look at him with those horrified, thunderstruck expressions, and Mannon wouldn't be reaching across Addison, trying to choke him.

The world seemed all wrong, like a forgery of the world he knew—the colors were blurred, the voices didn't sound right, his head and arms and legs felt numb, and everything was happening too fast or too slow, he couldn't tell which. There was a blur in the air over Addison's head, like a large, swift bird, and a loud splintering crack as the limb of a tree exploded behind them.

"They've seen us. They're coming!" someone shouted. Everyone broke into a run as the trolls stormed toward them. Patch looked back and saw their heads cresting the overlook, and their arms reaching up to clamber over the edge.

As Mannon ran he brought the horn to his lips and blew. Not the single long note that would have signaled, "Come finish them off," but three sharp bursts: the warning cry. The trolls thundered after them, plucking rocks from the snow and slinging them as they advanced.

Patch felt his jumbled senses clear as he ran. He could have easily outraced the others, but he slowed so they would not fall behind. They rushed down the hill toward the road, and more stones soared over their heads and between them, some careening along the ground and shearing sheets of bark from the trees they struck. He heard the trolls behind them, grunting, roaring, and barking, and heavy Mannon puffing as he ran. Then Ludowick shouted, in a voice suddenly cracked with emotion, "Go! To the horses! *Don't look back*, just go!"

They came to the road and turned toward Dartham. Five of the mounted soldiers were coming back for them, each leading another horse for them to ride. As they raced toward each other, Patch's blood turned icy cold as he heard Mannon cry, "Where's Gosling?"

Patch and Addison turned to look. Only Mannon and Ludowick were behind them. Mannon stopped and took a step back toward the hill. Ludowick seized his arm as he ran by and pulled him toward the horses. "Keep running! *Run!*" he screamed, and Patch saw tears streaming down Ludowick's face.

Mannon resisted, pulling his arm free from Ludowick's grip. The trolls came out of the forest and onto the road, just a hundred feet away. Some lumbered toward them, while others searched for more stones to hurl.

"He's gone, Mannon. He was next to me, and then a stone came, and he was gone," Ludowick shouted, and

Mannon staggered like a drunkard. Ludowick steadied him, then tugged his arm, and Mannon stumbled to his horse, his face slack. They mounted and raced away, leaving the bellowing trolls behind. The horses ran for a mile before Addison threw up his hand and they stopped. Addison whirled his horse around to face Patch, who bowed his head and stared at his hands.

"Milo insisted we bring you along, against my advice," Addison said, his voice shaking only a little. "So I trust you'll tell him what happened here today—and how we lost our chance to destroy the trolls. Or perhaps you'd rather take the road back to Crossfield." He spurred his horse and rode alone toward Dartham.

Patch closed his eyes, and his shoulders hitched. He heard another horse come near, and Mannon's voice, shattered by grief, came to his ear. "Gosling's life, thrown away to save a fool. I'll get you for this, apprentice. If I see you again, I swear I will." Patch heard Mannon's horse move on, the others following behind.

Patch waited. When he opened his eyes again, he was alone on the road.

CHAPTER 7

When the thump of the hooves could no longer be heard, Patch slid off his horse and vomited in the snow. He flopped on his back and drew his sleeve across his mouth. He cried out to Gosling, "I'm sorry!"

A sound caught his ear, and he looked up to see his horse trotting away without him, following the others down the road toward Dartham, already disappearing around a far bend in the road. *Oh, Mannon would have loved that,* he thought, and the mocking voice echoed in his brain: *Perhaps you'll remember to tether your horse next time!* He rolled over and pounded the frozen ground with his fists until it hurt too much to go on. He got to his hands and knees, then stood on wobbling legs.

Which way? he wondered. To the north were the trolls. To the south was Dartham, a shame he couldn't bear to face, and a knight who'd sworn to murder him. Neither way would do. *Home,* he thought. *I'm going home. Wish they'd never found me. Wish I'd never left.* He walked through the trees and onto the frozen lake.

Patch trudged across a dead landscape that an artist could have rendered by mixing only black and white paints. Gauzy sheets of snow curled and swept across the surface of the lake, revealing here and there the cracked gray ice below. The sky was an ugly leaden bowl clapped down over the world, spilling tiny flakes that were just now reaching the ground. The only visible color was on the cloak that Patch wore, a beautiful garment embroidered with purple. But the purple reminded him of the king and Dartham and Gosling, and he would have thrown the cloak aside if he didn't need it to keep him warm. The same went for the boots, the gloves, and the other fine gifts he'd received.

The town of Shorham was somewhere on the other side. From there Patch could pick up the same road they'd come down. He'd follow it all the way back, up the river, past Half, and on to Crossfield and the little tailor's shop.

He stopped, listening to a sound that was cutting through the whining breeze. He lowered his hood to hear it better.

"Hallooooo!"

Patch turned to see a tall, thin figure coming toward him, lifting his knees absurdly high as he ran and waving madly. When Patch recognized the fellow, he rolled his eyes and groaned.

"Hallooo! Oh, it's him, it's really him! What luck! Hoo ha!" Simon still had the troll's rope knotted around his waist, and it trailed thirty feet behind him. When he reached Patch, he lifted him off the ground, hugging him, and began to twirl. "My hero, my prince, my savior!" He planted a wet, loud kiss on Patch's cheek.

Patch slapped at the fool's shoulders and snarled, "Simon—stop it! Put me down—no, we're going to fall—" And they did fall, because the rope had wound around their legs as Simon spun.

Simon sat up, looking at the rope and scratching his head. "Where'd that come from?"

Patch kicked the loops from his legs and stood up. "The trolls tied you up, you half-wit! You dragged that rope a mile across the lake."

Simon snapped his fingers. "I think you're right! Wait—*what* did you call me?"

Patch grimaced. "I'm sorry, that was an awful thing to—"

"You called me *Simon!*" Simon gasped and clapped his hands to his head. "The hero knows my name! How can this be?"

"I'm not a hero," Patch said.

Simon kept his hands on his head, but his face grew serious. "Are you saying the wine *wasn't* poisoned?"

Patch winced. "No, it was poisoned all right, but—"

Simon dropped to his knees and seized Patch's hands. "Then I would be dead if not for you." Patch wrestled his hands out of the fool's grip and stepped back, out of reach. Simon grinned up at him like a puppy.

"Well," Patch said, "how'd you get away from the trolls?"

"They forgot all about me when they charged after you. What tempers they have! Why, once they—hold on! Halloooo there, *halloooo!*" Simon jumped to his feet and waved gaily at another approaching figure, a man on a horse.

"I'm in the middle of a lake," Patch muttered. "What is everyone doing here?" He just wanted to be left alone on his way back to Crossfield.

A soldier of Dartham approached, a thick-necked young man who peered down at Patch with a satisfied look on his face. "You're the apprentice, aren't you? Patch Ridling? I have orders to bring you to Dartham."

"Sorry, that's not me," said Patch.

"It isn't?" said Simon, utterly confused.

The soldier eyed Patch doubtfully. "Come on, you must be him. How'd you get that cloak then? That's royal purple, a gift from the king. I was told you'd be wearing it."

"Found it," said Patch through gritted teeth.

"I never find *anything,*" Simon said, with his lower lip thrust out.

The soldier looked behind Patch, toward the shore. "Looks to me like you came from the very spot where this Patch was last seen." Patch turned and saw the incriminating tracks in the snow.

Simon put his hand to Patch's ear and whispered, "Are you *sure* you're not Patch?"

Patch stared back at the soldier with red-rimmed eyes. "I'm not going back," he said.

The soldier jumped nimbly off his horse and loomed over Patch. "Son, our orders were clear: 'Track down the apprentice and bring him back.' And I don't mind saying that there's a generous reward for the man who finds you. So you're coming with me, even if I have to tie a rope around you and drag you through the snow." He cracked his knuckles.

"What fun!" shouted Simon, leaping up. "Can you tow the both of us? You can use my rope!"

The soldier looked at Simon from the corner of his eye, and back at Patch. Patch shrugged. "Don't ask," he said.

The soldier led his horse and walked with Patch, down the lake toward Dartham. Simon skipped alongside them. He whistled and laughed and told the soldier how Patch had saved his life. "Yes, heard all about that," the soldier said, looking at Patch and shaking his head.

Simon began to sing, loudly and badly, some nonsense song that Patch had never heard, nor wanted to hear again:

Catanese

"Listen to the hound
'Cause he smells the fox's blood
When he's running through the mud
And he makes his happy sound
Bark, bark, bark bark bark,
Bark, bark, bark bark bark!"

As Simon's song grew in volume and strayed further and further from any detectable melody, Patch noticed the soldier's jaw working from side to side and a thick vein emerging on the side of his neck.

"Listen to the cat
As she prowls around the house
Till she catches master mouse
And she leaves him on the mat
Mew, mew, mew mew mew
Mew, mew, mew mew—"

Suddenly Simon snapped his mouth shut like a trap door. The soldier was holding a gloved fist an inch away from the fool's long nose. Simon's eyes crossed as he stared at it.

The soldier curled his lip high on one side. "Listen, friend. That's an awful song. And nobody asked you to come along, anyway. So why don't you just shut up and leave us alone?"

Simon threw his long arms straight up in the air. When the soldier backed away, he remained in that position, as if frozen.

The soldier and Patch walked on. The tiny flecks of snow blossomed into broad, complicated flakes, and a soft new carpet of white collected under their feet.

"Look, can't you let me go? Why does the king want me back, anyway?" Patch said.

"The king? Who said anything about the king?"

CHAPTER 8

They stood in front of the gatehouse in the cold after-noon light. The outer portcullis was up, poised above them like fangs ready to strike, and the heavy doors stood open. "Found him, constable," the soldier called up.

A man with a round red face and a mustache that drooped past his chin looked down from the parapet above the gatehouse. "Be right down."

The constable appeared on the other side of the open gate, holding a small leather pouch and a bundle of brown material under his arm. He gave the pouch to the soldier, who shook it to hear the metallic jingle, grinned, and strode away with a happy bounce in his step.

The constable turned to Patch and unfolded the cloth. It was a hooded cape. "Put this on, young fellow. And draw the hood close around your face. Someone around here has pledged to kill you on sight."

Patch followed the constable into the courtyard. He breathed easier when they turned right, away from the knights' barracks and past the main entrance that led to the great hall. They walked around the frozen fishpond and circled a low stone building that sat next to the keep, with smoke puffing from a chimney in the tiled roof. Someone was waiting at the door. It was a small figure, also hooded, and as they drew close Patch saw the face of a girl. He turned to look at the constable, but the man was already ambling back across the courtyard to the gatehouse, looking casually to his left and right to see if he'd been watched.

"What . . . who . . . ," Patch blathered, but the girl shushed him and pulled him behind her into the building.

This was the kitchen of Dartham, as warm as a summer day and filled with smells that made Patch's mouth water. A baker was thrusting bread into a wide-mouthed brick oven with an inferno deep inside, a cook tossed vegetables into a cauldron hanging over an open fire, and another woman was plucking the feathers off a fat headless goose. They stole a glance at Patch and the girl and quickly looked away, as if they'd been instructed not to notice any strange visitors who passed by. The girl led Patch briskly through the room. When they reached the door at the far end, she turned to give him a closer look, her eyes flickering from his face to his feet and back. Then she pushed the door open, and they were out in the cold air again, under a covered walkway that led to a door in the side of the keep. Now Patch could see why he'd been taken this way: It was the most concealed approach.

Directly before them was an archway that led into the great hall. The girl turned down a parallel corridor instead. She took a torch from a bracket in the wall. Patch followed her up a tightly spiraling windowless staircase, where frost clung to the stone walls and twinkled in the light of the flame.

They emerged into a new corridor above the great hall and stopped when they came to a tall door. The girl rapped on the door three times, pushed it open, and gestured for Patch to go inside.

Patch stepped into the room and pushed back the hood of his brown cape. The room was small, comfortably furnished, and warm. There was a window filled with real glass, in hazy colors that warped the afternoon light. There was a canopied bed, unoccupied, thick with quilts and blankets. A small fire cast an orange glow on the walls, and there were three chairs in front of the fire. A familiar white-haired figure sat in one, bathing in the warmth, sunken and hunched. His shallow breathing was the only sound in the room.

"Will Sweeting?" Patch asked quietly, stepping closer. "You sent for me?"

"Not him, Patch." A woman stepped out from the corner of the room behind Patch. "I sent the soldiers to bring you here."

Patch saw the long raven hair and the slim band of gold around her forehead. "I saw you. After the council."

"Do you know who I am?"

Patch cleared his throat. "The . . . queen?"

She nodded. "Cecilia."

Patch opened his mouth, realized he didn't know what to say, and closed it again. Cecilia smiled. "I heard what happened. I worried what became of you. Especially when your horse came back without its rider."

Patch lowered his head. "I just thought I should go home. After the trouble I caused . . . and Gosling . . ."

The queen took his hand. "Come and sit by the fire." She took the seat beside Will Sweeting, and Patch took the third chair. "This is his room," she said, patting the old man's arm. Sweeting stared into the flames, his head bobbing gently. His breathing fell silent for a moment, then resumed, a little weaker than before. "Be strong for me," Cecilia whispered to him, squeezing his arm. "Stay with us a little longer, old friend."

Patch said, "He was a real hero, wasn't he?"

"Oh, yes." The queen pointed to the wall beside the hearth. A wide strip of heavy white cloth hung there, yellowed with age and frayed along the sides, hanging from a buckle that was looped over a nail. *A belt*, Patch realized. Words had been written in red thread along its length, in uneven stitches that betrayed the exhilaration of the young man who wielded the needle. Patch tilted his head to read the words aloud: "Seven at one blow."

Cecilia smiled at the old man. "Do you know the story, Patch? Young Will swatted seven flies that landed on his bread and jam, and he embroidered that belt to celebrate the deed. But people thought he'd slain *men*, not flies, and took him for a great warrior. Before long, Will was asked to battle dangerous foes—giants, even. And with courage and wit, he turned out to be a brave little tailor indeed. He became a valued adviser to Milo's father, and then to Milo. It is only in the last few years that he has begun to slip away from us.

"At first these spells of his, this wakeful dreaming, came once in a great while. Then they grew longer and more frequent. Now he is lost to us more often than not. Only on the rarest occasion does he lift his head and speak. But when he does, you realize that he is always listening." She patted the old man's hand. "A real hero, as you said. But you've been a hero yourself, Patch."

"Not me."

"You saved your friend, at the bridge in your little town."

Patch shook his head. "I didn't save anyone, Your Highness."

"You didn't kill the troll?"

"I guess nobody knows that part of the story," Patch said wearily. "I killed the troll, all right. But Osbert—my friend, the fellow on the bridge with me—he died anyway. Just an hour later. He was very sick. We buried him on a hill, just outside of the town." Patch slid off the chair and sat on the floor. There was a poker leaning against the hearth. He used it to prod the logs, sending crackling sparks into the air. "So I didn't save anyone. I didn't accomplish anything. That's why . . . that's why I wanted to help, with the trolls. I wanted to do something right, without something going wrong."

Cecilia sat beside him on the floor, crossing her legs and smoothing her long dress around them. "Look at me, Patch," she said.

Patch met her gaze, staring into eyes that were both green and brown, both compassionate and wise. "It seems to me you accomplished much on that bridge," she said. "You saved Osbert from a far worse fate than the one that took him. You stayed and fought for him, so he knew he was loved. How proud he must have been. What more could someone offer a friend?"

Patch drew his knees up to his chest and wrapped his arms around them. "But I've messed things up badly now. You should let me go home, Your Highness. Before anyone else gets killed because of me."

"You can go home if you want, Patch. But know this: That *was* a good plan you had. You couldn't have known what would happen, what would go wrong."

Patch groaned, remembering the awful turn of events that began as the fool was led out of the troll's cave. Then he sensed something, a quiet thought that until then had been drowned out by his head-splitting despair. "Hold on," he said. "Isn't it strange that the trolls would think to have someone taste the wine? And just a day after they killed Constancius and drank all the wine without a second thought? They're supposed to be stupid creatures. It's almost as if . . ."

"As if someone warned them?"

"I know, it doesn't make sense. Why would anyone do that?" Patch prodded the logs again with the poker. "You know what I think? I think it's that Hurgoth."

"Hurgoth?" the queen said, crinkling her nose.

"The leader of the trolls. He's smarter than the others. You should hear him talk."

"But is he clever enough to suspect a trap?"

Patch shrugged. "Maybe we were too obvious. Sending another wagon right down the same road. Maybe Hurgoth *is* that smart. Maybe he's behind all of this, leading the trolls so far from the Barren Gray. I just wish that we knew more about them—that we could get close to them, spy on them." He dropped the poker suddenly and clapped his hands to the side of his face.

"What, Patch?"

"Simon!"

"Simon?"

"The fool—the troll's wine-taster! He was their captive, for a day at least. And he got away somehow when the trolls attacked us. Maybe he heard something, saw something. We have to find him!"

The queen stood. "Stay here and keep my old friend company—perhaps he will speak to you again." She went to the door and opened it, and the girl who had led Patch to the room stepped inside.

"Emilie, go find the constable, dear. Patch, there is something else I must do now. When the constable arrives, tell him how he might find this Simon of yours."

Patch sat in the chair next to Sweeting and gazed at the fire. After a while he called the old man's name, but there was no response. "The queen says you're always listening, so let me tell you what I think," Patch told Sweeting. "You said you heard clues. Well, I've been remembering what Griswold told us about the trolls. I have this strange feeling, like the answer is right in front of us, but I just can't figure it out. It's all so confusing. The trolls are so strong—why do they stay in the Barren Gray? I always heard they don't like the sun, but we've seen them in the sun. Is it the warmth they hate? No—fire doesn't hurt them; it only sends them into a rage, so it can't just be the warmth. And what about the troll that Griswold said started beating itself on the head, then dropped dead? Or the troll that chased the little girl toward the meadow, then turned around and ran, terrified of something? What does it mean? I don't understand—"

There was a knock on the door, and the constable came into Sweeting's room. He said loudly, "Hullo there, Will," and sighed as the old man kept staring at the embers. He turned to Patch. "So young man, I'm told there is someone else to find?"

"His name is Simon, sir. The last time I saw him we were in the middle of the lake," Patch said. "He's very tall, and thin, and he's . . . well, he's not like most people. . . ."

The constable tilted his head to one side. "Wild

yellow hair, tongue hanging out of his mouth, wearing about seven shirts, one on top of the other?"

Patch blinked at the constable. "You've seen him?"

"Seen him? The madman showed up at the gatehouse right after you. Been telling us to let him inside so he can find his 'small friend,' his 'little hero'—is he talking about you?"

Patch's head shrank between his shoulders. "I suppose he is."

"He's an entertaining fellow, at least till he starts to drive you crazy. Tell you what—I'll find a place to keep him until Her Majesty calls for you."

After the constable left, some time went by before the door opened again. Emilie and another servant came in. Emilie signaled for Patch to follow her, while the servant stayed behind with Sweeting.

Patch and Emilie passed quietly through corridors and down staircases, keeping out of sight. At last she opened the door into yet another room, where the queen was waiting. Patch was going to greet her, but what he saw in the room struck him speechless. It was a sewing room of some kind, with tailor's tools spread out across many a table. There was bolt upon bolt of cloth, in more textures than he'd imagined existed, and a glorious riot of hues that a rainbow would envy, with spool after spool of thread to match.

"Thank you, Emilie, you may go," the queen said. She

looked at Patch. "We needed a quiet room to speak to your friend. I thought you might appreciate this one."

"Oh, yes," Patch said. There was a scrap of lovely gold cloth lying on the floor. He picked it up and rubbed it between his fingers. "I—I just wish my master, John, could see this. He'd think he was in heaven."

"Choose any color. No, choose three. And I will have them sent to your master."

"Three! Honestly?"

"Honestly," she said, smiling.

There was a noise outside, an absurd and familiar voice talking far too loudly. The door opened and the constable appeared, holding Simon by one arm, steering the fool through the threshold. "Oh, *another* delightful room," he said, gawking. His gaze fell upon Cecilia, and he squinted at her. "And exactly who are you supposed to be? Ouch!"

The constable had pinched Simon's arm. "That's the queen, you simpleton!"

Simon's legs turned to liquid, and the constable had to seize him around the waist to keep him from collapsing. "The queen . . . ," moaned Simon, swooning. The constable scuttled about to keep the fool upright, and they seemed to be dancing awkwardly together. Patch dragged a chair over and slid it behind Simon's knees. Simon's head flopped backward, and when he saw Patch standing behind him, he sprang to his feet and hugged him. Cecilia watched all this with enormous eyes and a hand held in front of her mouth.

Simon clapped Patch on the back and wept with joy. "It's you! My dearest, dearest friend in the world! What did you say your name was?"

"It's Patch, Simon. Now sit down, the queen and I need to talk to you."

"The queen," Simon moaned again. His eyes rolled up and he slumped into the chair.

Cecilia took one of Simon's hands and clasped it between hers. "Welcome, friend," she said. "I am so glad you came. The king needs your help." Simon raised his head and looked at the queen. Eyes bulging with awe and mouth stretched wide, he looked like a frog.

"The king needs *me*?" he said. "The king needs Simon Oddfellow?" His eyebrows rose so high they disappeared under his unruly stack of straw-colored hair.

"Yes, Simon. We all need you. You may be the most important man in the kingdom right now. Patch and I have questions for you. I want you to listen carefully and think about what you learned while you were a prisoner of the trolls. Will you do this for me?"

Patch marveled at the serenity in the queen's voice. It was like hearing the wind sweep across a field of wheat, or a brook splashing through a stony bed. And while it was Simon that the queen was trying to soothe, Patch felt some of his own anguish melting away. Even the constable, who was clearly worried for the queen's safety with this odd character in the room, relaxed enough to take his hand off the hilt of his sword.

Simon straightened up in his chair, put his hands on his knees, and nodded solemnly. The queen looked at Patch, ready for him to begin.

"Simon," Patch said, taking her place in front of the fool, "when did the trolls capture you?"

Simon scrunched his features together, concentrating. "Why, last night, I'm wandering about, and I find some folk keeping warm around a fire. So I start to entertain them. And suddenly, they scream and run away. So I shout, 'Sorry, I haven't had a chance to bathe for a while!' But then there's this hot breath on the back of my neck, and I'm picked up and stuffed into a sack. Well, I have a merry ride for a while, bouncing all about. Then I'm dumped out, and find myself surrounded by trolls!"

Patch turned to the queen. "So they captured him last night. *After* the plan was made to poison the wine."

"You must have been frightened," Cecilia said to the fool.

"Frightened? I was confused! That was the strangest audience I ever had. I drew pictures for them in the dust. They gathered around, and they seemed quite interested, and suddenly one of them hit me so hard I rolled over six times! The same thing happened when I sang my song. One moment they're laughing and the next, *pow*! They hit me again!"

"You sang for the trolls?" Cecilia asked, smiling.

"Oh, yes," Simon said, rising from his chair. The constable stiffened and prepared to draw his sword again.

Simon cleared his throat and put the splayed fingers of one hand on his chest. "Would you like to hear it?"

"Simon, I don't think—," Patch began, to no effect.

> "Listen to the hound
> 'Cause he smells the fox's blood
> When he's running through the mud
> And he makes his happy sound
> Bark, bark, bark bark bark,
> Bark, bark, bark bark bark!
> Listen to the cat
> As she prowls around the house
> Till she catches master mouse
> And she leaves him on the mat
> Mew, mew, mew mew mew
> Mew, mew, mew mew mew"

"Simon, please stop," Patch pleaded.

> "Listen to the bees
> 'Cause they must be making honey
> When they're sounding rather funny
> As they buzz about the trees
> Bzz, bzz, bzz bzz bzz
> Bzz, bzz—"

"Simon!" Patch snapped, poking the fool on the shoulder.

"That's just when the trolls hit me!" Simon said, sounding wounded.

"Small wonder," the constable said from the side of his mouth.

Patch rubbed his temples with his thumbs. "Sit down again, please, Simon."

"Simon, did you overhear the trolls talking? Did they say why they are here?" asked the queen.

Simon crossed his arms. "Well, my queen, I hardly think I should be snooping into anyone else's business."

"Simon, these trolls are dangerous—you have to tell us anything you heard!" Patch said.

"Oh, I see—well, I don't think any of you are in danger. It's somebody named 'Dartham' they're after."

The queen gasped. Patch dropped to one knee in front of the fool and clasped his arm. "Simon. *This* is Dartham. The castle you're in now. Where the king and queen live, and where they rule over the kingdom."

Simon's face lit up with recognition. "Ooooohhh! Then we're in a great deal of trouble, because I heard one of them say, 'Tear Dartham to pieces.' And I thought, 'I wouldn't want to be that Dartham fellow!'"

"When, Simon?" The queen's voice was suddenly toneless. "When will they tear Dartham to pieces?"

"I don't know, my queen. They're waiting for something before they start."

The queen looked to Patch. "Waiting for what?"

Patch shrugged. "Simon—the big troll named Hurgoth, the one that had you tied to the rope—is he the leader?"

Simon nodded briskly. "Oh, yes—that Hurgoth does most of the talking. He's the one that talked about Dartham, about waiting for something. And when the others start to grumble, he sets them straight, knocks them right on the head."

They kept asking Simon questions, but the fool had no more useful information for them. The queen asked the constable to take Simon to the kitchen for something to eat, and to reward him with warm clothes, boots, and a small pouch of gold coins.

"You were right, Patch," she said as soon as the door was closed. "And the king must know of this. He is holding another council right now. You should go and tell the court what we have learned."

Patch clutched the front of his shirt. "Me? Please, Your Highness—I can't! They all hate me because of what happened. Addison told me to leave. Mannon wants me dead!"

"Patch, we cannot wait. You must go, now."

"But won't it mean more if the queen tells them?"

Cecilia turned her back to Patch for a moment. When she turned to face him again, her jaw was set and there was a fiery glint in her eyes. "Patch, there are important men in this kingdom who don't like to perceive any weakness in their monarch. And if it were known that I could sway Milo, that he would look to his queen to help him through a crisis, then some of those men might lose respect for their king. No matter how honest or good or wise or fair a man he might be. And we must not let that happen."

They stared at each other for a long moment, the queen and the tailor's apprentice.

"You're always there, aren't you? Behind the curtain, listening when the king has his councils," Patch said quietly. "When the king goes for his walk before making a decision, he goes to see you."

"You must never speak of this," Cecilia said.

"I never will, Your Highness. But—you were there, when Griswold was speaking. And you heard everything he said?"

"Yes . . . ?" she replied, inclining her head.

A notion was growing in Patch's mind. Just a seed of an idea at first, but within seconds it was fully blossomed. He closed his eyes. *Was it possible? How long would it take to get ready? Could it really work? Perhaps . . .*

"Griswold said their eyesight was weak, didn't he?" he asked the queen. "And their tempers—he said they lose control when someone puts the flame to them, burns them. Didn't he?"

Cecilia narrowed her eyes. "What are you thinking about, Patch?"

Patch raised his fist and shook it. "Killing Hurgoth!"

CHAPTER 9

Patch peered out from the archway in the side of the great hall. Almost everyone who'd been present at the first council was there. Even Will Sweeting was in his familiar seat by the fire, perhaps hearing everything, perhaps hearing nothing. A queasiness fluttered in Patch's stomach as he saw the empty place next to Mannon, who sagged in his chair with a lost look in his tired, bloodshot eyes.

A page entered the hall and brought a folded note to the king, who once again sat at the center of the table in the tallest chair. The conversation slowed and stopped as Milo took a long time to read it, with a hint of a smile coming slowly to his face. He stood to address the others, tugging at his garments to smooth the creases.

"Well. This is a day for unexpected guests. Someone will be joining us now, and I trust he will be treated fairly when he appears." Mannon looked up, realizing that Milo had directed the comment toward him. His brow furrowed, and anger simmered on his face.

"Come out, Patch," the king called out, still watching Mannon. Patch stepped into the room, and all eyes turned toward him. He was just ten paces from the table, but suddenly walking felt like a forgotten skill. He crossed the space with his arms swinging awkwardly out of rhythm with his legs.

"So you have important news for us. We will hear from you in a moment, young apprentice," the king said. Milo had spoken to him warmly when they first met, but now his tone was as cool as the ice that hung from the sills of Dartham. "But first, we have word of a stranger, also claiming to bear important news. Please have a seat." Patch hoped nobody heard him gulping. The only open chair was the one between Mannon and Addison. Addison stared at him, as inscrutable as always. Mannon's nostrils had flared wide, and his meaty fists were threatening to wrench off the arms of his chair. Without another glance at either man, Patch went to the empty chair and sat.

The large doors to the great hall opened, and two of the king's soldiers escorted a long-haired, bearded man into the room. *A hunter*, Patch thought. His outer cloak and leggings were made of deer hide. An empty sheath for a long hunter's knife was at his belt, and a quiver with no arrows was strapped to his back; his weapons would have been taken from him before he was allowed before the king. A scar, long since healed, ran down the side of his face. It began at his temple and passed all the way down to his chin, leaving tracks where no whiskers grew. When the hunter drew close to the king, he dropped to his knees and bowed his head.

"What is your name, sir?" Milo said sternly.

"Clovis, Your Majesty."

"Well, Clovis. I am told that you have information concerning the trolls. And that you will tell it only to me."

Clovis kept his gaze on the floor. "Well, Your Majesty . . . when a man learns something as important as this, he hopes for some reward. For bringing it to your attention, that is."

Milo put one elbow on the table and leaned forward. "But you would be helping your kingdom and your neighbors, who are in danger. That would be reward enough for most men."

"There would be some satisfaction in that, to be sure, Your Highness," said Clovis, shifting his weight from knee to knee. "Pardon me for saying, but you can't blame a fellow for wanting to get something for himself in the bargain, a little silver in his pouch for when times get lean."

Addison gave the hunter a reptilian stare. "Perhaps," he said, "you should think less about the reward you will earn for your information, and more about the price you will pay for your greed."

Mannon began to push himself up from his chair. "And perhaps I can be the man to exact that price," he growled.

"Sit, Mannon, sit," the king said, rapping his knuckles on the table. "Master Clovis, I'm told that I am a patient man—too patient, even. But now I have reached my limit. Tell us what you came to say."

"Well," said Clovis, his glance darting around at the hostile faces around him, "two days ago I was hunting in the forest, north of the lake. I was on my way home, following my own tracks through the snow. Along the way I heard some unearthly sounds. Low talking and laughing, but not by people, you understand? I crept up to see what it was, and there's a pack of trolls before me, ten or more. But among them was something else I didn't expect to see."

"Which was . . . ?" said Milo.

Clovis cleared his throat and wiped his palms on his leggings. "I've come such a long way, Your Highness. Could've stayed in my woods, never left at all."

Basilus, the king's steward, appeared at the kneeling man's side, holding a goblet on a silver tray. He said, "Wine for the king's honored guest?"

"Thankee," Clovis said. He wrapped his fist around the long stem of the goblet and brought it, shaking, to his mouth. "Your Highness," he said, drawing his sleeve across his lips after a deep gulp, "forgive me if I'm just a good-for-naught scoundrel. But do you know, I've never owned anything of value in my life until I possessed this bit of intelligence. Is it so wrong I should profit from it?"

Milo rolled his eyes and gestured toward the two soldiers. Each of them reached down and clamped a hand on the hunter's shoulders.

"Wait, I'll tell!" Clovis cried. A pained expression came to his face, and Patch thought the rascal might be feeling remorse for his blackmailing ways. Clovis opened his mouth again, but no words came out, only a strangled croak. His eyes bulged, and he doubled over, as if a knife had been plunged into his belly. He rolled onto his side as the soldiers looked down in alarm. The silver goblet rolled out of his hand, making a graceful arc across the stone floor.

Addison was the first to reach him. He kneeled beside the fallen man, lifted him by the shoulders, and turned him to look into his eyes. "What's the matter? What is it?" Clovis was barely aware of him. Then his neck went slack, and his head rolled to one side. A drop of reddish liquid trickled out of the corner of his mouth.

Addison looked at the goblet, still rocking back and forth on the floor. "Basilus?" he said, raising his head.

Patch looked up and down the room. Basilus was gone.

"Poison," Ludowick said.

"Poison? My steward, a murderer? What on earth is happening here?" cried Milo.

"Your Highness, we must find Basilus. Learn why he's done this," said Addison.

"Yes—everyone, search the castle! Alert the gate-house! Find Basilus!"

There was a great thumping of boots and the screech of chairs shoved aside. A moment later everyone was gone—soldiers, guards, knights, and nobles. Only Patch and Will Sweeting were left in the room, with the corpse of the hunter lying on the floor growing as cold as the stone. Patch stared at the dead man, aching to know what poor Clovis had seen, what he could have told them.

Poisoned wine, thought Patch, shuddering. *My suggestion.*

He remembered the queen, and her hidden place at the back of the great hall. He walked there and went behind the curtain. The chair was empty. Of course, she would have left to avoid being discovered when the knights began running in every direction. He stood for a moment, wishing he could talk to her, wondering how he could find her.

Or maybe, Patch thought, he should join the search for Basilus. It might redeem him in the eyes of the king, Addison, Ludowick, even Mannon. But the castle was large, the corridors were many, and the hiding places were countless. He stepped back out from the curtain. *Where would I run if I were Basilus?*

A hint of motion across the room caught his eye. A tapestry hung on the wall, stretching from floor to ceiling to keep the cold and damp of the stone walls at bay. But it was swaying, almost too subtly to see, as if it had been given a gentle push. Patch watched, and the motion came to a stop.

You hid there, Patch thought. *Until the knights left. Then I stepped behind the curtain, leaving only Will Sweeting in the room. And then where did you go?*

There was an archway to the right of the tapestry. Had any of the knights even gone that way? Patch dashed across the room and through the opening, where the corridor ended in a staircase. How far down the stairs went, Patch could not tell; darkness swallowed everything beyond the fourth step. He ran back to the great hall, grabbed a candlestick from the table, and came back to the top of the steps.

He sniffed the air. There was a familiar scent rising from the darkness. *Cheese,* he thought. And other smells—like barley or oats, and the yeasty aroma of ale.

"Patch," a voice said behind him, and he almost shrieked in surprise. It was Cecilia. "What are you doing?"

"My queen! Did you hear what happened?"

"Yes. The poison. That poor fellow. What could he have been about to say, to make Basilus kill him?"

"I can't imagine," Patch said. "But I suppose we know who warned the trolls about the wine."

The queen nodded, then saw Patch looking down the stairs. "That leads to the storeroom for our provisions. You don't think he's down there, do you, Patch? He would be trapped—there is no way out except these stairs."

"But he could never get out of Dartham with all the gates patrolled. So maybe he found a place to hide awhile—with food and drink. Until it's safe to sneak out." Patch started down the first two steps.

"Wait! You can't go alone!" the queen said, tugging at him. "I'll find help." She gathered up her long gown and raised it above her ankles so she would not fall as she ran.

Patch watched her until she was out of sight. He moved cautiously down the stairs again. *Can't wait*, he thought. *It's my chance to make good.*

There was a door at the bottom of the stairs. Under the handle was a keyhole. He pulled at the handle, and the door swung open with a loud creak. *Shouldn't the provisions be locked up?* he wondered. *But of course, the king's steward would have a key.* He held the candle before him and stepped into the room.

His heart was pounding and a sprinkling of sweat had erupted on his forehead, but even through his fear he could appreciate the wonderful smell of this room, the scent of basil and pepper and salt and dozens of other herbs and spices. The room was twenty paces wide and at least forty deep, as far as the light of his candle informed him. It was crowded with sacks of grain, casks of wine and ale, jars of honey, bushels of beans and barley, barrels of salted fish, meats hanging from hooks, and a great many wide wheels of cheese.

"I know you're here, Basilus," Patch called out, his voice

ringing against the stone walls and low ceiling. He peered through the gloom. Something shone out brighter than the rest of the objects there, an incongruous thing. It was a staff of polished white wood. Patch remembered it—from the night he first arrived at Dartham, when Basilus met them at the door.

The faintest sound came from behind him—it might have been a sharp intake of breath or the rustle of a robe—but it was enough to make Patch leap forward. He heard the *whoosh* of something sharp and narrow slice through the air. The back of his linen shirt tore, and he felt a line of pain, blazing hot, just below his shoulders.

Patch whirled about. Basilus was there, holding a gleaming meat hook. The steward's calm demeanor and regal posture were gone. Now he crouched with his teeth bared, his nostrils flared, and sweat trickling down his temples. "Don't move—I won't hurt you," he said, stepping toward Patch. It was such an absurd thing to say, as he raised the hook to strike again, that Patch almost laughed.

"Help is coming," Patch said, sliding backward.

"I don't believe you," Basilus whispered, creeping closer. He stabbed at the air to the right and left, forcing Patch straight back until he bumped against the sacks of grain piled against the wall. There was no more room to retreat. He opened his mouth and took a deep breath.

"Don't scream," Basilus warned. Patch did not; he blew the lungful of air at his candle, putting out the flame. Everything fell into blackness. Patch dropped to his haunches, hearing another *whoosh* in the space he had left, and sprang like a frog to one side.

Basilus grunted and cursed. Patch could hear him stabbing at the air in every direction. "If I don't kill you, I'll make sure the trolls do," the steward hissed. There was a crash as he blundered into a stack of something that fell to the ground, and he cried out in pain. Patch heard him whimpering and moving again, toward the door. He followed the sounds, keeping a safe distance between them. *I'm not losing you now*, he thought.

Patch heard the steward's feet on the steps. As Basilus mounted the stairs and moved closer to the light, Patch followed. Then came the thump of heavy boots in the main hall and the sound of shouting: "Where's the boy?" "Through there—down the steps!" "Bring torches!"

Too late Patch realized that Basilus had turned and was rushing back down the stairs. He pressed himself against the wall, but the steward's feet caught on his as he passed. Patch heard Basilus yelp as he fell, an ugly thud of something hard striking stone, a sound like a tree branch snapping under the weight of snow, and the harsh music of the meat hook clattering down the rest of the steps.

A flickering orange light filled the stairway. Addison came first, with a torch in one hand and his sword in the other. Three soldiers followed, peering over his shoulder.

"I found Basilus, my lord," Patch said. For a moment

he'd forgotten the pain where the hook had sliced his back. Now it blossomed again, much greater, and he felt a spreading warmth and dampness.

Addison walked past him, to the foot of the stairs where Basilus was crumpled in a heap. He knelt by the steward and brought the torch close.

"It would have been well had you kept him alive for us to question," Addison said.

CHAPTER 10

"**B**etter a thousand enemies at my gate than one hidden in my house," said Milo, shaking his head. He stood by the roaring fire, with a hand on old Will Sweeting's shoulder and his back to the rest of the people in the great hall.

Patch hovered by the door. Many of the knights were gathered here again. They sorted themselves into groups and spoke in hushed tones. Addison sat away from the others. His sword was still drawn, and he leaned on it, brooding, with the hilt propping up his chin and the tip slowly turning, grinding on the floor.

The men began to notice Patch. Faces turned his way, curious or suspicious or resentful. There was Mannon, but trying to meet his eye was like staring into the sun.

It seemed to Patch like he couldn't get anything right. Yes, he'd found the traitor. But now the traitor was dead and could answer no questions. What did Basilus have to do with the trolls? What was the hunter about to say, that he had to be so cruelly silenced? Was only Basilus involved, or were there others?

An hour before, the queen had brought Patch a physician who washed the cut on his back, smeared it with an ointment that naturally made the pain ten times worse, and wound a cloth around him. She hovered nearby while the physician worked, but Patch was afraid to look her way. If he'd only listened to her and not gone down the stairs by himself, Basilus might have been captured alive. *Would* have been captured alive. But he was too anxious to help, too eager for redemption.

Cecilia did not scold him, though. When the physician was done, she only patted his hand and said, "Go and tell them now, Patch. This cannot wait. I will be listening."

Now Patch looked around the room at the important men. He glanced at the long curtain behind the table and pictured the queen in her hidden chair. It made what he was about to do a little easier.

He walked toward the king. The conversations withered, and heads swiveled to track him as he approached the hearth. "Your Majesty," he said. Milo turned and stared at him. The friendly glint in the king's eye was gone; his youthful face looked ten years older.

The king's eyebrows crinkled together as he seemed to remember something. He patted his pocket and reached in to pull out a small folded parchment. He opened it and read it. Patch recognized the note that the page had delivered just before the hunter was poisoned, before

Basilus broke his neck on the stairs. It was Cecilia's note, the one Patch had watched her write: "Let the apprentice speak, my love. And listen well." Milo sniffed, smiled briefly, and tossed the note into the fire.

"Well," the king said. "What do you have to say?"

Without mentioning the queen, Patch told the court what they had learned from Simon Oddfellow: that the trolls were planning to tear Dartham to pieces, that Hurgoth seemed to be in charge, and that they were waiting for something to happen before the attack would begin.

As he spoke, the men gathered around to listen, forming a half-circle in front of the fire. Except for Addison, who was still perched on his chair, leaning on his sword.

Ludowick spoke first when Patch was done. "Are you certain about this, apprentice?"

"I am, my lord," Patch said.

Mannon crossed his arms and scowled. "Hold on—are we really going to take the word of a boy and an imbecile?"

"What if he's right, though?" another knight said.

Other men began to cry out, shouting to be heard over one another.

"Even if he is, what can we do to stop it?"

"I heard about what they did at Half!"

"What did Basilus have to do with all this?"

"We need more soldiers!"

"Now that the traitor's dead, perhaps they'll go away!"

Milo raised his hands. "Quiet!" he shouted, and the

clamor died at once. The king rubbed his closed eyes with the tips of his fingers. He turned his back to the men once more and stared into the flames. "Addison," he called loudly, without turning around.

Addison looked up, roused out of some weighty thoughts. "Yes, my king?"

"Have you ever known our kingdom to face a greater threat?"

The question surprised Addison. "Not like this. Not ever."

"Not ever," Milo repeated, turning around. "So we can't play games anymore. We can't and we won't." He pushed through the half-circle of men, strode past the table, seized the curtain, and gave it a mighty pull. It tore away from its long wooden rod and fell to the floor. The men in the great hall gasped as the queen was revealed, sitting in the hidden chair.

Cecilia was halfway out of the seat and poised to run, but froze when she realized that she'd certainly been seen. She lowered herself deliberately into the chair again and looked out at the men, her eyes wide and glistening. Milo went to her and held out his hand. "No more hiding, Cecilia. No more notes. No more secret meetings. This is all too important. I need you by my side. My wisest, most trusted adviser."

Cecilia stood and allowed the king to lead her to a seat at the table. The rest of the men stood about, clearing their throats and glancing at one another. They turned to watch as Addison stood up, walked to the table, and sat next to the king. Ludowick sat down next, and Mannon lumbered over and sank onto a chair. And then the rest followed. There was no sound except the wooden feet of chairs scraping against stone.

Patch was still standing by the fire. He glanced down at Will Sweeting and could swear he saw a hint of a smile on the old man's mouth as he sat there, gently rocking.

All eyes were on Cecilia, and she began to speak. "Good men of the court. We know that there will be an attack on Dartham. We know not when, but we must assume that it will come before long. So whatever we do, it should be done soon."

As she spoke, the queen looked at each of the men in turn. "Like you, I am deeply troubled by the treachery of Basilus. And I yearn to know what the hunter would have told us. But we have learned something that may be our salvation.

"Do you remember what Griswold taught us? He said that trolls are solitary creatures. For them to invade as a group is not merely unusual—it is unprecedented in all our chronicles. Something is holding this ugly horde together. And from the fool Simon, who was once their prisoner, we may have learned what it is: Hurgoth, the wisest and strongest of them. He herds the rest like sheep. And perhaps, without the shepherd . . ."

"The flock would disperse," said Milo.

"You're suggesting we destroy Hurgoth?" Addison said. "But how?"

"We have an idea," said Cecilia. "That is, the apprentice has an idea. Tell them, Patch."

Patch gulped as every head in the room turned his way.

The shirt that Basilus had torn was still stained with blood but the rip was healing under Patch's nimble fingers as he sat beside the hearth in the great hall after the council was adjourned. His needle pierced the fabric, crossed under the tear, and came up on the other side. He pulled the needle, tugging the thread and drawing the sundered edges together. It felt good to be sewing again. The rhythm of it, as familiar as breathing, kept his mind off the peril he would soon be walking into.

Patch was so absorbed that he was caught off guard when a shadow fell over him. He flinched like a cat, half expecting to see Mannon looming overhead with sword drawn. But it was Ludowick.

"Sorry to startle you," Ludowick said.

"It's all right, sir," Patch replied. He put his needle down and stared up at Ludowick.

The knight shifted on his feet and cleared his throat. He paused for a moment and then sat beside Patch on the floor, with his back against the stone wall of the hearth. Patch glanced around the hall and saw that they were not entirely alone in the room. Cecilia stood at the far end, along with Emilie and two other handmaidens. And Simon was there entertaining them—he had picked up a chair and balanced it on his chin.

Ludowick said, "Well. You've had your share of adventures since you arrived, eh?"

"Misadventures, sir," Patch replied.

Ludowick gave him a wry smile. "I spoke to Mannon. Pointed out that Gosling's death was not your fault. If anyone was to blame, it was the villain Basilus, who surely warned the trolls about the poison. That's why everything went wrong."

"What did Mannon say?"

Ludowick shrugged. "Not much, frankly. You have to understand that Mannon and Gosling were the best of friends. Mannon's in a rage and itching to make someone pay for his loss. Until we meet the trolls in battle, you are the easiest thing to blame. Now, Mannon will be with us tomorrow; we may need his strength. Until then I would steer clear of him if I were you. Same goes for your friend," he said, rolling his eyes toward Simon. The fool was losing control of the chair and running back and forth beneath it to regain its balance, to the handmaidens' alarm.

"I wish Gosling was here," Patch said quietly.

"As do I. As do we all." Ludowick sniffed and rubbed his sleeve under his nose. "Do you remember a particular troll, the red-brown monster?"

Patch remembered that troll all too well, one of the

tallest after Hurgoth. "His skin looks like red clay—and he's got a long fang sticking up on one side of his mouth."

Ludowick nodded, his expression grim. "That's the one that did it. Gosling and I were running together. Then the stone came through the trees, and that was the end. There was nothing I could do. But I turned back once as I ran, and saw that red devil heading right for Gosling's body. And he was smiling. *Smiling*."

They sat side by side for a time. At the other end of the hall Simon was trying something new. His mouth was gaping wide, and he was rapping at his teeth with his fingernails, shaping his lips to produce different musical notes. The queen and her handmaidens exchanged bemused glances.

"Sir, I was wondering . . . what do you think of my plan?" Patch asked.

Ludowick raised his eyebrows. "For a boy with no apparent luck, you're counting on plenty if you expect this to work."

"Do you know how Lord Addison feels about it?"

"Apprentice, if you ever find out how Lord Addison feels about *anything*, be sure to let me know. He is a muted man. You wonder if a heart truly beats under that stern flesh. But as for your plan, he is out there himself, supervising the preparations. Consider that an endorsement."

Ludowick yawned and rose to his feet. "Time to get what little rest I can, I suppose." He crossed to the far end of the great hall, stopping to bow to the queen before leaving. The queen nodded and smiled at him, then turned her attention back to Simon.

When Patch saw that Simon was lying on the floor at the queen's feet, he shot to his feet and began to walk briskly to the other end of the hall. *Oh no, please no*, he thought, and he began to run.

Simon had contorted himself into a knot, like the first time Patch had seen him in Shorham, that village by the lake. The fool was on his back, tucking his ankles up behind his neck. His long arms reached around his knees and back again, so that his chin rested on his interlaced fingers, just above his buttocks.

And now, horror of horrors, the queen was reaching down to squeeze the fool's nose. "Your Highness, no!" Patch cried, but it was too late. Simon farted again, a barbaric blast of improbable volume that echoed between the wide walls of the great hall.

Cecilia staggered backward, and her hands fluttered up before her mouth. All she said was, "Oh! Oh!" before her handmaidens, recovered from the shock, seized her arms and bustled her through the nearest door.

"Simon, are you mad?" Patch said, almost moaning. "What have you done?"

As Simon sat up on the floor, propping himself with his arms behind him, his ridiculous smile withered. His mouth curved down and his bottom lip began to tremble. And then, from just around the corner where the queen and her ladies had disappeared, an unusual noise came, a kind of sputtering. After a moment, Patch realized what it was: the sound of a woman trying desperately not to laugh. Then she surrendered, and a merry, merry laughter rolled down the corridor, high and musical and lovely, with a sudden uncouth snort in the middle of it all, and then endless giggling as the handmaidens joined their queen.

The familiar, foolish grin returned to Simon's face, and he waggled his shoulders. "What I do best," he replied.

CHAPTER 11

"The weather favors you, Patch," Addison said, brushing snow from his shoulders.

"It ought to help, my lord," Patch said. He looked at the countless flakes drifting down from the heavens in a slow, dreamy chaos. "Covers things nicely."

Addison nodded. He watched as the men he'd supervised, all bearing saws and hatchets, trudged out of sight down the road. He glanced up at the hillside, where the trolls' cavern lay. "You don't have to be the one, you know. I had volunteers."

"I don't want anyone else hurt because of my crazy ideas, my lord. Besides, I'm the fastest."

"Is that so?" Addison nearly smiled, and then his face became its usual stony self. He handed Patch the heavy lantern. "Then we might as well begin. Before it grows too dark. Be careful. If you stumble once . . ."

"I know. I won't. See you soon." *I hope*, Patch added inwardly. He stepped out onto the road.

Almost immediately, he heard a familiar voice in the distance. "Hoo ha! Hallooo, Patch!"

"Not now, Simon," Patch groaned. The fool skipped toward him, waving his arms. Patch motioned for him to go back and raised a finger to his lips. It seemed like a miracle when one of the king's soldiers darted out from the trees, clapped a hand over Simon's mouth, and pulled him off the road.

Patch rolled his eyes and took a deep breath. He crossed the road and began to climb up through the forest. Whenever the wind gusted, snow would tumble off the high branches of the trees and cascade down. The new snowfall was several inches thick, deep enough to slow him down—but not too much, he hoped—when it was time to run.

He headed for the same ledge that they had used to spy on the trolls on their previous, tragic visit. As before, he crawled up on his stomach and peered over the side.

The trolls had been busy. They'd built a fence around the mouth of the cave, and dozens of sheep and pigs huddled in the enclosure, as far as possible from the three trolls squatting at the cave's entrance.

Hurgoth was not among them. Patch began to panic. Hurgoth *had* to be there; everything depended on him. After a minute, Patch saw him emerge and stretch his arms in the last rays of the afternoon sun. He was easy to spot—taller than the rest, with chalky gray skin, wearing that small pack on his back.

Patch's mouth went dry, and his heart was leaping inside his chest. He had been sure he could do this, but now every part of him felt suddenly weak, and it seemed impossible to take the next step. But he thought about Gosling, and a hot rage welled up inside him. He got to his feet, lifted the lantern, and shouted, "I have a message for Hurgoth!"

The trolls turned toward the sound of his voice. The three sentries hissed and began to run toward the ledge where Patch stood.

"A message from Basilus—he sent me in his place!" cried Patch.

The creatures were just a few strides away when Hurgoth called out to them. "Leave him to me!"

The ceatures stopped. One of them reared his head back and spat at Patch. A dreadful blob arced through the air and splattered on the face of the ledge just below his feet. The troll snickered at him, a black pointed tongue flickering out between his teeth.

Hurgoth was coming. His legs were longer than most of the other trolls', and his powerful arms swung as he strode over, covering the ground with worrisome speed.

Hurgoth's chin was at the same level as the ledge. Patch took a step back, worried that those long arms and clutching fingers might come up for him. "Keep your distance," he said. He had not stood so close to a troll since he'd faced the old blind creature on the bridge at Crossfield, and he was reminded of how strange and small the eyes were: tiny quicksilver orbs with black dots in the center, nestled in deep shadowy sockets. Out from their corners trickled a thick yellow liquid, like a constant stream of tears. "The weeping trolls," old Griswold had called them. Patch caught a whiff of the sickly sweet smell, the scent that revived memories of Osbert and the bridge and the ruined town of Half, and he wondered if that yellow stuff was the source.

"What do you mean, a message from Basilus? I don't know any Basilus," Hurgoth said.

"Don't play games, Hurgoth. I bring a message from your friend, the king's steward. But it's meant for *your* ears, not theirs." Patch jerked his head toward the three trolls lurking behind Hurgoth.

Hurgoth cocked his head to one side for a long moment. "Back in the hole," he growled over his shoulder. The three trolls turned and walked grumbling toward the cave.

"Well?" Hurgoth said. "What is this message?"

Patch patted his pocket. "I have it here somewhere. Oh—what's this?" He pulled out a yellowed object that looked like a thorn from a giant rose stem. It was as long as his hand was wide. He held it up for Hurgoth to see. "Look familiar?"

Hurgoth squinted at the thing. Then his gaping nostrils flared wide, and his lip curled high on one side.

"I remember now," said Patch. "It's a tooth from that miserable old troll I killed." A low growl rumbled up from Hurgoth's throat like distant thunder. The massive troll edged a little closer to the ledge. Patch saw the beast's elbows and knees bending and his back arching, and he knew Hurgoth was getting ready to pounce. *That's fine*, he thought, both encouraged and terrified. *The madder the better.*

"I thought you had a message," Hurgoth said, still coiling.

"I do. But it's not from your pet, Basilus, after all. That traitor is dead. The message is from the king. And he says to haul your ugly carcasses back home, or he'll—" Hurgoth sprang for the ledge, bellowing, heaving his bulk into the air with surprising agility. Even though Patch was expecting it, he nearly didn't get away in time. He felt the vibrations as Hurgoth's claws raked across the stony ledge with a sound like screeching falcons.

Hurgoth's leap had carried him waist-high to the ledge, and his legs hung awkwardly below him. He was perfectly vulnerable to what Patch planned to do next. "And here's a gift from King Milo too!" Patch cried, and he flung the lantern just as the troll pushed himself up. It struck his broad chest and shattered, and the oil burst into flame.

Hurgoth howled. It wasn't the low guttural yell that Patch could feel in his ribs, but a high piercing screech that made him clap his hands over his ears. The troll pounded at the flames that covered his chest. He crawled the rest of the way onto the ledge and flopped into the snow, and a sizzle of steam rose out from under him. Then his head came up, and his silver eyes, which seemed to have doubled in size, found Patch. He scrambled to his feet and smashed his fist into a nearby tree. The tree splintered, and the snow on its branches flew a hundred feet in every direction. Hurgoth threw his head back and screamed again, clawing madly at the air over his head. Then he came for Patch.

Perhaps Patch was imagining it, but he could swear that he heard a distant voice shouting, "Stop! You'll be killed!" There was no time to ponder it, though. He ran downhill, along the tracks he'd made on the way up, hopping over stones and winding through trees. He looked back to see how close Hurgoth was, and caught a glimpse of the monster, insane with rage, wrenching a huge limb off another tree as he ran by and carrying it for a club.

Patch had been certain that he could outrun Hurgoth. He thought he'd have to slow down, even pretend to stumble and fall, to keep the chase close. But the snow clung to his feet, making him work harder for every step, and the distance between them began to shrink.

The sun was behind him as he ran east down the slope, toward the road. Hurgoth's long shadow crept closer. Patch hurdled a fallen tree, and Hurgoth took it in stride, closing the gap a little more. Patch looked over his shoulder and caught a fleeting glimpse of the troll, grinning and scowling, spouting steam from his nostrils, swinging the club over his head.

Perhaps it was the blood he'd lost from his wound, or the extra effort from churning through the snow, but Patch was tiring. There was a lightness in his brain, and the cold air burned his lungs.

They came out of the forest and onto the road. Patch dashed straight across and into the trees on the other side, heading for the safety of the snow-covered lake.

"You won't reach the lake in time, tiny one!" Hurgoth roared. Patch saw the dark shadow under his feet, the elongated shape of the troll's powerful arm wielding the club. Suddenly the silhouette of the club parted from the shadow of the hand, and Patch darted left just before the enormous branch that the troll had thrown crashed beside him.

He was through the trees and onto the wide flat ground that led to the lake. Far ahead still were the landmarks that had stood at the water's edge—the tiny fisherman's shack and the boat hauled up on the shore.

Now under his feet he saw the dark shadow of Hurgoth's head, and he knew the troll must be just a stride behind. Hurgoth's churning, stomping feet struck a low evergreen tree. It broke off clean and flew spinning over Patch's head. He hoped the troll didn't notice just how easily the tree had lifted out of the snow, or that its trunk had been neatly sliced with a saw.

Again Patch heard that voice shouting, "Stop, stop!"

But it wasn't a distant voice, he realized. It was near, but curiously muffled.

The shack was still fifty feet away, but the chase was nearly over. Half of the troll's shadow was in front of Patch, and he watched as the black forms of the arms came toward him from both sides. He felt something nudge his shoulder, and he knew it was one of those thick nails at the end of Hurgoth's fingers. Panic coursed through him, and with a final surge of energy, the last that could possibly remain, he raced onward just a little faster.

The shack was steps away. Patch ran straight for its open door. "That miserable hut won't save you!" Hurgoth cried, panting. In those final steps Patch once again heard that odd voice calling, "Stop! Stop! You'll be killed!"

Patch dove into the shack, sliding on his belly all the way to the far wall. If the plan was to work, it would happen now. Even as he turned to look, he heard a shattering crack as the ice broke under Hurgoth's feet. The troll dropped into the black water, his dense bulk pulling him down as if he were made of iron. Hurgoth opened his mouth to howl, and icy water surged down his throat as the head slipped under the surface. Jagged sheets of ice bobbed where the troll had stood only a second before.

Patch rolled onto his back with his arms spread wide, gasping for air. Men ran out from the corners of the shack—Addison, Mannon, Ludowick, and more—carrying battleaxes and maces and spears, shouting and laughing. They surrounded the hole, eager to beat at any large gray hand that came up groping for purchase. "Come on," Mannon shouted into the icy waters. High over one shoulder he waved his mace, a bladed club heavy enough to crush armor. "You ugly demon! Just try coming up!"

Patch joined them at the edge, clasping his hands behind his neck to open his aching lungs wider. He peered into the dark water, trying to see through the jumble of broken ice. Great quantities of air bubbled to the surface. For a moment, that was the only sound, until Patch heard a familiar laugh and saw Simon skipping toward them from the shore, clapping his hands over his head. "Hoo ha! A remarkable ruse!"

"The fool speaks true," Ludowick said, looking around to admire the trap that Patch had conceived. The little house that stood by the edge of the lake had been lifted up by the king's men and hauled out over the depths, and the boat was carried there as well. Trees and bushes were sawed down and stuck upright in the snow-covered surface, so that the troll might believe he was still on the shore and venture out over the lake. Just in front of the house, the thick ice was weakened with axes in a broad circle, so the troll would fall through. They had plumbed the depths: The bottom of the lake was over thirty feet below.

"Ho! Look here!" Mannon shouted. Near the edge of the hole, the water bubbled anew, and a shape struggled toward the surface. "What the devil?" Addison said, as a figure, too small to be a troll, came sputtering up.

It was a man. Mannon dropped the mace and hauled him out onto the ice. The stranger drew his knees up beneath him and coughed up water. Addison strode over, waited until the choking stopped, then put his boot to the man's side so that he flopped onto his back, shivering.

The knights looked down at the man. Then they turned their gaze toward Addison. There was no sound except the chattering of the man's teeth. "Tell me I'm not seeing this," said Ludowick. Simon had arrived, and his eyes goggled and his chin drooped as he stared at the wet man. Then he began capering around, singing, "Rotten fish! Rotten fish! Caught ourselves a rotten fish!"

Patch was thinking about how Hurgoth always wore that pack on his back—the only troll to do so. He remembered the muffled voice he'd heard at the end of the chase. And how Hurgoth would pause before answering. Suddenly, all of these things made sense. "This man was inside Hurgoth's pack," he said, hardly believing it himself. "Whispering in Hurgoth's ear! Telling him what to say. Telling them all what to do."

Everyone was still staring uncomfortably at Addison. Patch didn't understand why until he looked again at the stranger. This time he saw the rust-colored hair. The narrow face. The sharp hooking nose. "Lord Addison, who is this?" Patch said. But in his heart he already knew.

"This rotten fish," Addison said, "is my brother Giles."

"But I thought your brother was dead," said Patch. "Killed by the trolls."

"Just as I did," Addison said.

"Addison," Ludowick said quietly. "I have to ask . . ."

Giles Addison raised his head from the ice and laughed. His lips had turned blue from the cold, and his voice quavered as his body shook. "Ask w-w-what, Ludowick, if he's mixed up in this? My forthright, upright, do-no-evil brother? The k-king's faithful servant? You give him too much credit. He lacks the imagination. Or the c-c-courage to seize what he wants."

Addison turned his back on his brother. He walked off to stand at a distance, leaning on his spear like an old man.

Mannon picked up his mace again. He put a boot on Giles's chest and pushed him flat on the ice. He held his weapon high. "Let me do it, Addison! Right here! I'll fillet this fish for you!"

"Then it will be you who brings ultimate d-d-doom to your k-k-king and kingdom, Mannon," Giles Addison said. "Are you sure you w-w-want all that royal blood on your hands?"

"What are you talking about? Your game is over, Giles."

"Look over there and tell me that again, Mannon."

Mannon looked—they all looked—and saw a second troll standing by the true shore of the lake. This one was not as tall as Hurgoth, but wider and thicker; his skin was white with veins of gray and black, like a living chunk of marble.

"Murok, you know what to do!" Giles shouted. The creature turned and stomped back through the forest, heading for the cave.

"What now, Giles?" Addison was coming back toward them, his hands balled into tight fists.

"Why don't you t-t-take me to your wise k-k-king, and see what he will do with me," Giles said. "After all, you have h-h-him to thank for this m-m-mess."

"Signal for the horses," Addison called. "We will cross the lake to get back to Dartham, so my brother's new friends cannot help him."

The men spurred their horses for the first half mile across the lake, leaving the giddy fool far behind.

Giles had his hands bound behind his back, and a rope was lashed between his horse and Mannon's to prevent his escape. He was still dripping wet and shivering, but no one offered him a blanket or cloak. Patch looked back at him, trying to make sense of this startling turn of events. How could a man like Giles get these monsters to do his bidding? One possibility occurred to him. And the more he pondered it, the more plausible it seemed. He pulled back on his horse's reins and allowed Giles to catch up. Giles gave him a dismissive glance, as if Patch were some kind of stray animal.

"I think I know why the trolls obey you," Patch said, as casually as he could. "You learned something about them when you went to the Barren Gray. You know what kills them. So they'll do whatever you say, to keep their secret."

Giles flinched. It was the subtlest, tiniest gesture, and it was gone an instant after it happened. But Patch was certain he'd seen it, and it made him sure his guess was right. Then Giles yawned and called ahead to his brother. "Goran, have you taught this boy no respect? I would normally whip a peasant who dared address me directly."

Addison spoke without turning. "That *peasant* was clever enough to slay Hurgoth and flush you out of your pathetic hiding place. Perhaps it is you who is not showing the proper courtesy."

"Interesting," Giles said, appraising Patch more closely. "Was that hole in the ice your plan, boy? The king's new pet, the tailor's apprentice? Oh, don't look so surprised. I'm well aware of you."

Mannon glared at Giles. "Of course you're aware. That snake Basilus kept you informed."

"I can't imagine what you mean," Giles replied, smiling.

Mannon reached over, grabbed Giles's collar, and pulled him within an inch of his own face. "What did you offer Basilus? To spy for you and guard your secret?"

If Giles was intimidated, he did not show it. He shrugged. "What we all want. A little barony to call his own. A little gold to ease his worries. Now let me go, you hairy toad, before I am slain by your breath." Mannon twisted the collar in his fist, pulling it taut around Giles's neck. Patch saw Mannon's chest heaving, and he knew the knight wanted to strangle Giles right there, or hurl him headfirst onto the frozen lake. But finally Mannon shoved Giles upright in his saddle again.

Giles stretched his neck and rolled his head from left to right. "You know, Mannon, the day may come when you beg me to spare your life. I wonder if I will forgive you?"

CHAPTER 12

The last light of day had slipped from the sky, and the great hall of Dartham was filled with shadows.

Giles sat, bound to a chair. Milo was there, and Ludowick and Mannon. Addison paced back and forth behind his brother. Patch looked at the brothers' faces, so similar in many ways. Both had rust-colored hair and arrowhead beards, dark eyes, thick brows, and narrow hawkish features. But the sum of those elements was so different on each brother. Addison exuded confidence, Giles arrogance.

"So, Giles," the king said, standing in front of the prisoner. "I sent you to the Barren Gray to learn about the trolls. Instead you enlisted them for your own devilish plans."

Giles stared coolly back. "Let us speak openly, Milo. You sent me to the Barren Gray hoping I'd be *killed* by the trolls."

"Don't be insolent, Giles," Addison said. "This is our king you're speaking to."

Milo leaned on the arms of the chair, close to Giles. "Is that what this is about, Giles? Petty revenge, because you felt slighted, threatened?"

"I don't think it was I who felt threatened," Giles said. Then the smirk faded from his lips, and his eyes locked onto some target beyond Milo's shoulder. Patch saw Cecilia standing at the far end of the great hall, framed like a portrait by an archway and illuminated by candles that her handmaiden Emilie was holding. He looked back at Giles and saw in those ink-dark eyes a chilling, ravenous expression. It was the way a wolf might stare at a helpless fawn. Patch had the strong urge to step between them and break the line of sight. Cecilia turned, her gown swishing, and moved past the archway and out of sight.

Milo had seen the look in Giles's eyes. "That was always your problem, Giles. Wanting things that weren't yours. But you're not getting what you want, not any of it. So you might as well tell us: Why did you lead those trolls here?"

Giles leaned back in his chair and resurrected his smirk. "I'm not ready to talk about that yet, Milo. I mean, *Your Majesty.*"

"Then why did you attack Half?" the king demanded. "What could you possibly gain from that?"

"It was time to feed my trolls. You would be astonished at how hungry those creatures get, Your Majesty. And to be honest, I was curious."

"Curious? About what, Giles?" Addison said from behind his brother's shoulder.

"About how strong they were, what they could accomplish. Do you know that it took only two of them to bring down that tower? Imagine what all of them could do to a bigger place. A place like Dartham, for example. The walls are much greater here, but still . . ."

Mannon stepped up beside Milo. He clasped the hilt of his sword and drew a third of it out of the scabbard. "Have we not heard enough, Your Highness? Let's end this now. Send his head to the trolls in a basket."

"That," Giles said, "would be a terrible mistake."

"What are you up to, Giles?" Milo said. "We know you were planning an attack on Dartham; the fool that you captured told us so. What were you waiting for?"

For a moment Patch thought Giles was opening his mouth to answer the question, but instead he yawned, and then smacked his lips and stared smugly back at the king. Patch could only imagine how angry Milo was, and how ashamed Addison felt.

A page entered the great hall and rushed to the king. He had to squeeze his message in between the gulps of air he was taking to catch his breath: "Beg pardon . . . Majesty . . . must come . . . now . . . trolls . . . at the gate . . . calling . . . for you . . .

"Watch him," Milo snapped to a group of soldiers,

pointing at Giles. He strode off after the page. Addison and the knights followed. Patch paused, wondering if he should go too. He glanced back at Giles and a prickly sensation shot up his spine when he saw the wicked man staring back at him. "By all means, join them, apprentice. Don't miss the show."

Patch pursued Milo and Addison and the knights as they left the great hall and ran toward the gatehouse. The courtyard was suddenly crowded with people; not soldiers or knights but ordinary folk, and many of them were weeping. More streamed in from outside the walls; not through the main gate, where the great wooden doors were barred tight, but through some of the smaller entrances on the other sides of the courtyard, where king's men waved them through.

Above the gatehouse Patch saw dozens of men lining the top of the wall. Some held torches, most of them had their bows ready to fire, and all of them stared at something outside the walls of Dartham.

There were rounded towers on either side of the gate-house, and within them were stairs that circled up to the top of the wall. Patch followed the knights, keeping a few paces behind in case he was not welcome. When he was halfway to the top, the stairs opened into the winch room on the right, and there he caught a glimpse of mighty chains wrapped around three large drums—one each for the drawbridge and the inner and outer portcullises.

Patch climbed on and paused at the threshold at the top of the stairs. He could not yet see what they were looking at, but he heard Ludowick gasp and Mannon grunt in dismay. He edged out carefully onto the parapet and crept a little farther down, ducking between two soldiers and peering through one of the regular gaps in the wall where archers would fire their arrows.

The trolls were there, not a hundred feet away. They had built a fire, and it was growing rapidly, the flames soaring higher than the thirty-foot walls of Dartham.

"Watch for flying stones," Mannon's gruff voice warned anyone who would listen.

Outside the walls, hard to see in the darkness, were sprawling fields and pastures and the village where hundreds lived, farmers and craftsmen and merchants and laborers. By the light of the fire, reflected on the white carpet of snow, Patch saw people still racing out of their homes and running for the safety of the castle walls.

The trolls made no move to attack. Half of them were facing the gatehouse, while the other six had their backs turned. *Watching for an attack from behind,* Patch thought. But then he saw how their arms were out of sight, as if the monsters were cradling something they didn't want the king and his men to see. He wondered what it might be, and supposed that he really did not want to know. *Don't miss the show,* Giles had said with a wicked glint in his eye.

The constable pushed through the crowd of soldiers

and bowed to Milo. "They said they wanted to see the king, Your Highness."

Milo walked to the edge of the wall. "You asked for the king. Here I am."

Murok, the marble-skinned troll that Giles had spoken to, stepped forward. He raised a thick finger and pointed at the king. "Let him go," he called up, in a rasping voice.

"Who—Giles Addison?" Milo answered. "He must pay for his crimes. And you and your horde should return to your home."

Murok growled something over his shoulder, and the trolls that had kept their backs to them turned around. Yes, they were holding something, and it was worse than Patch could have imagined. Each held a child around the waist with a monstrous hand.

The children wailed as the trolls lowered them to the ground. The hideous creatures each lifted a foot and lowered it again, with their heels in the dirt and their long clawed toes pinning the children down. Murok stared fiercely up at the king. "Let him go," he repeated, "or we stomp."

Milo put his hands to his face and bowed his head. Cecilia appeared behind him from the gloom of the staircase. She walked to Milo's side and hugged his arm. He looked at her, and his face seemed to have gone gray. "My queen," he said, "we both know what must be done." He called to the constable. "Get the prisoner. Bring him to the gate."

Patch heard Mannon nearby, nearly overcome with anguish. "Let Giles go? After what he's done? We can't!"

Mannon stepped toward the king, but Ludowick threw an arm across his chest. "What else can we do, Mannon? Will you stand here and watch this?"

Milo leaned over the wall and shouted down to the trolls. "He is coming. Don't hurt those children, or I swear your fate will be a thousand times worse than Hurgoth's!"

The trolls roared with laughter and jeered at the king. "Who cares about Hurgoth?" called Murok, in a voice like rusted iron cogs gnashing together. "Your stupid tricks won't work again. Give us your prisoner!" Murok reared his head back and howled, and the rest of the trolls howled with him, drowning out the cries of the children.

The king went into the tower again. Patch ran to the inner edge of the wall and saw Milo reappear in the courtyard. The king waited there as a smirking Giles Addison was led out of the castle, surrounded by guards. Giles's hands were manacled behind his back, and irons were around each ankle with just enough chain between them to allow him to walk.

Someone stepped up behind Patch. It was the queen. She crouched low, so the wall would keep her mostly hidden in case Giles should look up.

Patch could just overhear the conversation in the courtyard below. "I should have executed you the minute they brought you to me," Milo said.

"Oh, but the children, the children," Giles replied, smirking. He turned his back to the king and shook the irons that bound his hands. "Take these off me."

Milo nodded to the constable, who produced a set of keys to free Giles's hands and feet. The king gave a signal to the men at the gatehouse. The rumble of the great drums turning and chains rolling came from the winch room, and the twin portcullises groaned upward. Four soldiers entered the passage, unbarred the front gate, and swung it open.

"You have your freedom again. I suggest you and your new friends enjoy it far, far away from here," Milo said.

"Hmmm," Giles said, rubbing his wrists. "I'll have to think about that. I must tell you, though, I'm not pleased about the cold bath your little apprentice arranged for me." He looked around the courtyard. "What—doesn't the queen wish to say farewell?" Patch felt Cecilia's hand grip his shoulder as Giles mentioned her name.

"The queen is sickened by the sight and sound of you," Milo replied. "As are the rest of us."

Giles laughed. "Perhaps I will see her again soon, anyway. Until then, Milo." Patch watched Giles disappear under the wall, and he went to the other side to watch him emerge outside the castle. Behind him he heard Milo shouting, "Leave the doors open for the children!"

Mannon was still on the wall. He clutched his head and moaned. "Murderer. Fiend. I can't believe we're letting him walk away."

Giles strutted away in no hurry. He stopped halfway across the drawbridge and peered down, examining the ditch full of frozen mud that surrounded the castle walls. He nodded and smiled as if something there pleased him. Then he walked out of the light of the gatehouse torches, through a pool of darkness, and emerged into the glow of the bonfire. When he reached the trolls, he turned to look back toward Dartham. He said something to Murok that Patch couldn't hear from this distance, and the troll chuckled cruelly. Then Giles walked off, and the trolls released the children and followed him.

One by one the children got to their feet and came weeping toward the gatehouse. A handful of soldiers had come out as far as the drawbridge. They held their torches high and waved the children on, urging them to hurry. Some were injured and limped badly. A young girl hopped bravely on one foot.

A murmur passed through the crowd gathered atop the wall, and men began to point.

One of the children, the smallest of them, was not moving. From where he stood, Patch could not tell if it was a boy or a girl. The child was lying in the snow, dressed in a simple long shirt that was not warm enough for this cold night. One of the trolls passing by noticed the child and stopped to look closer. And then two more came back. "What you got there, Gursh?" one said to the first troll. They loomed over the child, bending closer and sniffing.

The child stirred and lifted up its head, and now Patch could see that it was a boy, fair-skinned with curls of golden hair. The boy saw the three trolls hovering over him and cried out.

The rest of the trolls were far away now. Giles either did not know or did not care what the three stragglers were up to.

The one called Gursh was the most savage-looking of the trolls. He was not as large as the others, only eleven feet tall or so. His dark gray skin was splattered with green blotches that resembled lichen. A white froth bubbled perpetually out of the sides of his wide mouth, giving him the appearance of a mad dog. He squatted beside the child and prodded with his finger. The boy screamed up at the troll, and Gursh bared his fangs.

Cecilia pushed between two of the archers and called down to the men on the drawbridge. "Help the child! You must go and help him!" The men looked up as the rest of the children streamed past them through the main gate. They stared at the three dangerous-looking trolls. None of the men looked eager to venture out.

The little boy tried to crawl away, but Gursh stabbed one sharp nail through the end of his shirt and pinned it to the ground.

"Help him!" Cecilia screamed, first to the soldiers on the bridge and then again to the men around her on the wall. "Help him!"

"Look," someone shouted. A lanky figure, dressed in

fine clothes and a hooded cloak, was dashing out of the dark fields toward the trolls. Patch saw something familiar about the jouncing, loose-limbed stride. Even before the hood fell away from the man's face and he saw the mess of straw-colored hair, he knew who it was.

Simon skidded to a halt in front of the trolls. He stuck one leg out before him, with the heel on the ground and the toe up, and bowed deeply. The trolls glowered at him, and a sound like a low angry purr rumbled up from their chests. Simon grinned, did a happy little dance, and picked his way through their legs. "Excuse me, old friend," he called up to Gursh, and heaved on the troll's wrist to lift his pointed nail out of the ground and free the child.

Gursh snarled and swatted Simon with the back of his hand. Simon rolled backward, with his feet flying over his head, and popped up again with a wild grin on his face. He teetered to the left and right, feigning dizziness, until he was close enough to gather the boy up in his arms. The child bawled, and Simon pretended to cry as well, rubbing his own eyes with his free hand. All the while he tried to find a way past the trolls. But wherever he turned, one of them moved in front of him. Simon feinted right and darted left, but Gursh's leg slammed to the ground, blocking his escape.

Murok's raspy voice roared over the fields. "You three—what are you waiting for?" When the three trolls turned to look, Simon ducked low and darted through the nearest gap—between Gursh's legs. He emerged on the other side, pushing the leather garment up and out of his way, with a disgusted look on his face. Gursh turned and swiped at Simon, but the fool was out of reach. The trolls snarled. One of them took a step in Simon's direction, then stopped and joined the others as they loped after the rest of the trolls.

Simon carried the boy through the snowy field and across the drawbridge, grinning happily with his tongue hanging from his mouth like a dog on a galloping cart. All along the wall, the soldiers cheered and waved their bows. Patch thrust his fists into the air and shouted Simon's name. He looked at the queen, and she was leaning with her back against the wall of the gatehouse tower, sliding down until she was sitting, smiling, and crying at the same time.

CHAPTER 13

Patch woke from a dream he could not remember. Last night he'd found it hard to sleep, after everything that had happened. So he turned his mind to the mystery of the trolls. Now that he was awake, he had the uneasy feeling that the answer had been there in his dreams but slipped away when his eyes opened.

And why had he woken up? A great snore reminded him. Simon was sleeping nearby. They had both spent the night in the great hall, near the warmth of the fire. Patch was not eager to sleep in the barracks, as Mannon's anger still simmered. Cecilia understood, and she had arranged for straw mats to be brought to the great hall for the two of them.

Patch chuckled as he looked over at the fool. Simon was hugging an enormous wheel of cheese, his reward for rescuing the boy. "The queen asked me what I would like," he'd said to Patch, "and I chose this!"

All the things Simon could have asked for, and he wanted

cheese, Patch thought. He'd never seen a person look more joyous than Simon at that moment, taking bite after enormous bite from the wheel. Even now, sleeping and clutching his cheese, the fool seemed utterly content. He must have woken up during the night and nibbled some more, because the cheese was oozing out from the corner of his mouth. The sight reminded Patch of the yellow stuff that trickled from the eyes of the trolls, and the sick-sweet smell.

He wished he could be as carefree as Simon, because the crushing weight of what might come was settling upon him once more. Giles Addison was free to command the trolls again. Soon he would bring them back to attack Dartham and depose the king. But when? Would this be the day?

"What is their weakness?" he whispered toward the ceiling. There was a vulnerability, he was certain about that. It explained how Giles had been able to seize control of the trolls, something no man had ever done. And it explained other things as well. The trolls seemed nearly invincible, so why had they never attacked like this before? Why exile themselves in a place as desolate and cold as the Barren Gray, when the pigs and cows and horses and people they loved to devour were so plentiful down here? And why were such ornery, solitary creatures suddenly banding together? His intuition had to be right: There was a well-guarded secret among the trolls, a secret that Giles had somehow learned.

Clues, Will Sweeting had said. *Don't ask why they're here, ask why they never came before.* Patch closed his eyes and imagined that all the bits of information that he'd learned from Griswold were the fragments of some broken vase. All the pieces would come together if he arranged them correctly and turned them just so.

They call them the stone trolls. The weeping trolls.

They prefer stony ground.

They are bolder in the winter than any other season.

A troll wouldn't chase a child into a meadow.

The rare troll that wanders down during the summer prefers to stalk at night.

People thought trolls were harmed by sunshine—but it isn't true.

A troll was once seen going berserk, slapping its head. Then it dropped dead.

The answer was there, so close if he could only put it together. It was a frustrating sensation, this *almost knowing*. It was like a sneeze that would not come, or a thread that stubbornly refused to pass through the eye of a needle.

Patch lay there arranging the imaginary pieces until the growing pressure in his bladder was too great a distraction. He got up, ran to the privy that was nearby, lifted the wooden seat, and relieved himself down the stone shaft. There was a narrow window in the little room. Looking out, he saw a small group of men walking across the courtyard. Two of them had a stretcher between them, bearing a body beneath a blanket. The king was walking beside them, his head bent low. They disappeared into the chapel.

Patch left the privy feeling uneasy, wishing he knew—or perhaps glad he did not know—who was under that blanket. When he returned to the great hall, Simon was bent over with his back to the fire, waving his naked buttocks over the simmering embers.

"Do you mind?" Patch said wearily, blocking the sight with one hand.

Simon hiked up his pants. "Chilly, isn't it! Like some cheese?"

"No thanks," Patch said. He had no idea what to do next. There was no council scheduled, no plan that he was aware of, nothing he was needed for. He picked up his cloak and left the great hall. He heard feet slapping the floor behind him and saw Simon running to catch up, with his cheese tucked under one arm.

In the corridor Patch saw Emilie, the queen's handmaiden. Her eyes looked red and swollen, and she was dabbing under her nose with a handkerchief. "What's happened, Emilie?" Patch said, dreading the answer.

"Last night," Emilie said in a halting voice, "Will Sweeting passed away."

"No," Patch said. Emilie swept past him, sniffing.

Simon's eyes grew moist, and his lips trembled. "Will Sweeting? Oh, this is terrible." He put his free hand around Patch and pulled him close.

Patch sighed deeply, wishing with all his soul that

Sweeting had awoken for them one more time, with one more piece of advice that might help them out of this dilemma. "Simon?" he said, his voice muffled against the fool's chest.

"Yes?"

"Do you know who Will Sweeting was?"

"I have no idea!" Simon sobbed. He dropped the wheel of cheese and hugged Patch with both arms, bawling on his shoulder.

Patch stepped into the courtyard, and the mild morning surprised him. It was not a spring day by any means, and his breath still formed a white plume in the air. But it was not like the bitter, freezing chill of the last few weeks. The keening wind was gone as well, and tendrils of mist sprouted from the snow. Perhaps this long winter might be ending at last. He pulled the mittens off his hands and stuffed them into the pocket of his cloak.

"There you are!" Simon said, popping out of the doorway behind him. "I turned around, and you were gone!"

Patch's shoulders slumped. "I know, Simon."

Simon looked confused for a moment, and then his smile returned. "Where are you off to?"

"To the chapel. To pay my respects to Will Sweeting."

"Then I shall go too!"

Patch squeezed his eyes shut. "With that cheese under your arm?"

Simon didn't seem to hear him. He was biting his

bottom lip and looking around the courtyard. "It looks like ghosts are everywhere," he said, and his legs began to quake.

"Don't be ridiculous, it's just the snow melting into the air," Patch said. The words came out too sharply, and he regretted it at once. He was about to tell Simon he was sorry, that Will Sweeting's death had rattled him, when a commotion arose at the gatehouse.

Three mounted men rode into the courtyard, ducking impatiently beneath the rising portcullis. One of them was Addison. He dismounted and handed the reins to a servant. "Hold the gate open until the people are inside, then shut it tight," he called up to the constable on the wall. Patch looked through the passageway under the gatehouse and saw them coming—more men and women and children from the sprawling village that surrounded Dartham. Some of them carried bushels of food and drink, some rode carts loaded with goods, and some drove oxen and cows and horses and pigs and sheep and goats and geese before them.

Simon squeaked like a little girl. "We're having a festival!"

"It's not a festival, Master Simon," came Ludowick's voice as he walked past them toward Addison. "They're taking shelter inside the walls. Preparing for a siege." *But there won't be a siege*, Patch thought, recalling the tower of Half that the trolls had torn down. Were the walls of

Dartham so much stronger? *Sieges take a long time. This will be swift.*

Milo emerged from the chapel, and he and Addison walked briskly toward each other. "Simon," Patch said, holding the fool by his arms and looking him in the eye. "I want to hear what Lord Addison is saying to the king. Please, please—stay here and don't follow me."

Simon's mouth drooped at the corners. "I suppose." He lifted his cheese and gnawed meekly at a fresh curve of the wheel.

Patch didn't arrive in time to hear Addison, but he saw the shocked look on Milo's face and heard him say, "*How* many?" And then high screams came floating through the open gate.

On the wall the constable shouted, "Run! All of you, run!" Villagers and their animals streamed in through the gate. Patch followed Milo and Addison as they ran for the gatehouse tower, pushing through the growing crowd. The constable's voice grew more urgent: "Forget the food, forget your animals! Pick up your children and run!"

Into the tower Patch raced, up the dark stairs that curved to the right. As he passed the opening to the winch room, he saw a soldier hefting a heavy mallet, poised to strike a peg that would allow the great wooden drum to spin freely, unwinding the chain and dropping the portcullis to the ground in an instant.

Patch stepped into the weak morning light. Once again archers took their places along the battlements. He saw an open place among them and ran to it. A moment later Ludowick came up and stood beside him.

Directly below, people still stampeded into the courtyard. They crowded and pushed each other on the bridge, and a few tumbled into the ditch and scrambled up the side to reach the arched opening of the main gate.

Patch looked out over the fields and the village. It was an eerie sight. Overhead he could see blue sky, but the landscape below was blurred by the rising mist. The fog was thicker outside the walls; after a few hundred yards, nothing was visible. But there were sounds—a dog howling, the squeal of a pig abruptly ending, low grunts and snorts. A lone duck waddled out of the fog, quacking absurdly. There was the growing stomp of heavy feet, and then dark shapes began to appear behind the curtain of white.

"Archers," Addison called out. "If the trolls attack, aim for their eyes." There were nearly a hundred bowmen along the parapet, and they all drew arrows from their quivers and fitted them to their longbows.

The shadowy forms were resolving themselves, but something about the shape of their heads looked different. "Armor—they've got armor!" one of the soldiers shouted. It was true. The trolls tromped out of the mist, and now they wore helmets that shielded their eyes, with only narrow slots to see through. Some, but not all, had crude armor covering their chests and backs. But that was not the worst of it.

There were more of them now. A dozen were already in sight, but other hulking shapes came into view, trolls that Patch did not recognize from the original band of twelve. They spread out in a line, forming a wall of gray that looked almost as daunting as the walls of Dartham. More and more appeared, until there were at least thirty of the towering beasts in a line two hundred feet across.

"That's what Giles was waiting for," Patch said.

"Reinforcements," said Ludowick.

One of the larger trolls stepped forward from the middle of the line. It was Murok, Patch realized. Even with the helmet on, Patch could tell who he was by the exposed skin of his arms, which looked like veined marble.

Giles Addison appeared over Murok's shoulder. He had been riding the troll's back in some sort of harness. "Are you there, Milo?" he shouted, with a cupped hand beside his mouth.

"What do you want, Giles Addison?" The king's voice boomed strong and clear, with an authority Patch had not heard until now.

"To discuss your surrender, of course!"

"Then you are wasting your breath and my time," Milo answered.

Giles laughed. "So say you now! But hear me out, my friends. There is no need for any more blood to be spilled. First, let me warn you: Get those archers out of my sight, and don't even think about sending an arrow my way. My trolls will attack at once with a ferocity you cannot imagine. Have you noticed how many more we are now? I was waiting for the others to arrive—they were busy getting our armor ready. We found a country blacksmith, and—er—*persuaded* him to fashion this armor. Do you like our helmets? I thought you might aim your arrows at their faces. After all, that's what I would have done.

"Now, hear my terms, Milo. And I must tell you, I have altered them since your dirty ruse on the lake. You've angered me, you and your apprentice. Before he nearly drowned me, I was planning to let all of your people go. All you had to do was unlock the door to your treasury and vacate the castle—leaving your crown on the throne before you left, of course. Exile would have been enough. But not anymore. Now, Milo, I expect you and that brat to surrender yourselves to me. So that I may treat you to a fine cup of wine."

A low laugh came from the trolls as one of them stepped forward and planted a wine cask in the snow beside Giles.

Patch glanced at Ludowick, who winced and nodded. "One of ours," the knight said.

Giles sat on the cask and smiled up at Milo. "The rest of your court can go free. With one exception. The queen stays here. With me."

Milo's mouth twisted with anger. Nearby, where the

constable stood, a pair of the archers still had their arrows notched in their bows. They held them low, out of Giles's sight behind the wall. The constable stared at the king without blinking, waiting for a signal. Milo gave the tiniest shake of his head: *No.*

"Forget this, Giles," Milo shouted. "The knights won't stand for it. The people won't stand for it. Wearing the crown won't make you king."

"You are right about that." Giles swept his arm toward the line of trolls. "Intimidation will make me king. So, Milo—do you accept my terms? The alternative is a brutal death for everyone inside those walls. I'm asking a small price, don't you think? Just you and a peasant boy?"

Milo's face turned purple, and he was about to shout back when Addison grasped his arm and whispered in his ear. Milo thought for a moment, nodded brusquely, and turned to address Giles once more.

"We will take some time to consider what you have said," he called out. Patch noticed the king's eye twitching.

Giles laughed. "Taking counsel from my brother? Such a cool-headed, steady fellow that Goran is. Let me guess—he advised you to buy some time, so you might better plan your defenses. Fine with me, if you want to play games. But there will be no escape for any of you in the meantime." He turned to the trolls and pointed right and left. A small group of the monsters stayed with Giles, but the rest began to move off, spreading out along the walls and vanishing into the fog.

"And one more thing," Giles called loudly to the men lining the wall. "You soldiers, you servants, you lesser knights. I'm sure some of you are secretly grateful that a new king will take the place of this spineless worm. Milo the Mild! I know you call him that when his back is turned. You'll welcome a king who doesn't spend so much time worrying about 'the poor folk.' A king who dreams of bigger things and a bigger kingdom. A king who knows how to reward the people who matter— those who protect the throne and fight for its glory.

"Remember this: If Milo hesitates to surrender himself and Dartham, you may want to give him a nudge in the right direction—if you understand my meaning. I will remember those who stand with me."

"Go to the devil, Giles Addison!" shouted an anonymous soldier near the far end of the wall.

Giles smiled. "And I will surely remember those who stand against me."

CHAPTER 14

Patch pushed the door of the chapel open and looked inside. Nobody seemed to be there, except for the cold body of Will Sweeting, laid out on a table near the altar. Patch stepped inside and pushed the door shut behind him. It closed as silently as it had opened.

He glanced around the room, its walls paneled with wood, lovely colored glass in the windows, and a high ceiling that rose to a point overhead. With a heavy heart, he walked between the rows of benches to where Sweeting lay and looked down at the old man. Sweeting's breath had been so weak, so shallow near the end. Patch supposed it had slowed and slowed until it finally just stopped, like a clock winding down. He was reminded of seeing his friend Osbert after he died.

A lock of gray hair lay across Sweeting's face. Patch brushed it to the side and smoothed it. "Will Sweeting. I wish we could talk one last time. I know the answer is there. I've thought about it, but I just can't figure it out."

"Do you know what I can't figure out?" A deep voice boomed out behind Patch. Startled, he spun around and fell backward against Sweeting's body. It was Mannon; he had been lying down on one of the benches, hidden between the tall backs until he sat up. Mannon leaned forward and looked at Patch from under those heavy black eyebrows. "Why you're still here. Wait—don't tell me, I can guess. You're waiting for a reward from the king. Like old Will Sweeting there earned. You're hoping to do something heroic, so Milo will grant you some scrap of land or a barony. Or a little sack of gold at the very least, eh?"

Patch felt his face grow warm and turned away from Mannon. *Is that the truth?* he wondered. In the back of his mind, had he expected that all this would eventually mean a gift from the king, some wealth or a title?

"Of course that's it." Mannon leaned back on the bench. "Well, apprentice, that man behind you was a giant killer. He actually *solved* problems. And that's the difference between you and him. It seems to me that every time you get an idea, it *creates* a problem. First Gosling dies. And now, though you've exposed the mastermind of this plan, you made Giles so furious that all of us in this castle may be dead soon. Humph."

Mannon hawked up something from the back of his throat and turned as if to spit. Then he realized where he was and swallowed it back down, grimacing. "Seems to me that if you've earned anything, it's a whipping. So here's an idea. Why don't you sneak away and go back to your worthless old master in your insignificant village? You're good at running, right?"

Addison's voice came from the far end of the room, by the door. "That is enough, Mannon." Mannon turned to argue but snapped his mouth shut when he saw Milo beside Addison. He shot a poisonous sideways look at Patch as he rose to his feet.

"Enough indeed," Milo said. "Don't blame the apprentice for our predicament. If you need to blame someone, you can blame me."

Mannon lowered his head. "Blame you? Never, my king."

"Oh, but this is all my doing." Milo sat down on one of the center benches and stared out through the colored glass in the windows. "Who do you think sent Giles to explore the Barren Gray to begin with? I knew he was dangerous, that he had his eyes on the throne. And my queen, for that matter. I thought it would be better to remove him from the things he coveted so badly." Milo smiled sadly at Patch. "And then I heard the story of a tailor's apprentice, slaying a troll on the bridge in Crossfield, and I had the sudden inspiration: Send Giles off to the Barren Gray! To map the land and investigate the threat of the trolls!"

Patch suddenly felt unsteady on his feet, listening to the king. *He got the idea from me? All this is because of me?*

Addison had one eyebrow lifted in a rare expression

of surprise. "So you sent Giles on a dangerous expedition. Hoping the trolls would solve the problem for you."

The king winced. "Mainly I wanted him out of the way for a while. But I admit: The thought occurred to me that if Giles somehow didn't make it back . . . it might be the best outcome for all concerned. Addison, I must apologize. I know this is your brother we're talking about."

Addison shook his head. "I need no apology, Your Highness. Giles has proved your point—he is every bit as ambitious and wicked as you supposed. And as for our predicament, you could not have guessed that Giles would somehow learn to command the trolls. Who could have?"

"No one. But here they are. And Giles knows what I was up to. So his incentive is doubled now. He's here for the throne and revenge . . . Patch, my boy, are you all right?"

Patch had slumped to the floor, his chin resting on his knees and his hands folded over his head. "It's all because of me, Your Majesty," he said. "None of this would have happened if Osbert and I had gone to the other bridge. Or if I hadn't fought the troll. You'd never have gotten the idea. I started everything."

"So you did," Mannon muttered. "Tell us, apprentice, were there ill omens the day you were born? Did a shadow cross the moon, or was a calf born with two heads?"

"Enough, Mannon!" Milo snapped. "Leave us!" Mannon stormed down the aisle and slammed the chapel door behind him.

Milo walked over to Patch. "Don't give it another thought, lad. I for one am glad we met. You do remind me of this old, old friend of mine." The king reached out and touched Will Sweeting's clasped hands. "Good-bye, Will. I had already begun to miss you, even before you were gone. There won't be time for a proper burial; I hope you'll forgive us that." Milo kissed Will's cold forehead and left the chapel.

Patch shut his eyes and stayed on the floor with his hands over his head. His heart felt weak and his brain felt numb. He heard a noise beside him and opened his eyes to see Addison sitting there, leaning on one hand and looking steadily at him with those dark eyes. There was a softness in his expression that Patch had not seen before, as if his features were ice under the first rays of sun.

"Patch, what do you think about our king?" Addison asked.

Patch took his hands off his head and folded them in his lap. He considered the question for a long moment. "I like him, Lord Addison. I think he's a decent man."

"Decent. That's the very word. I like him too, Patch. I'm glad he's our king. You can talk to him like any other man. He's actually an ordinary fellow. And that makes him almost extraordinary.

"You see, Patch, becoming a monarch usually does something to a person. A regular man can have a simple, harmless fault. But make him a king, and that fault grows wider and deeper, and it becomes a vast, gaping flaw that brings suffering and ruin to all his people.

"A greedy man is just a nuisance, like that innkeeper Bernard; but a greedy king gathers all the wealth for himself while his people go hungry. A violent man brawls with his neighbors until someone throws him in jail; but a violent king wages unjust wars, even against his own people. A suspicious man doubts his brothers and mutters against strangers; but a suspicious king sends even his loyal friends to the gallows. Do you wonder why I'm telling you this?"

"You want me to know why your brother must not become king."

"Yes. It's more important than you can imagine. Giles Addison is all those things. He is greedy, violent, and suspicious. Worse yet, he has a wounded heart, which a man like Giles cannot abide. You see, he was spurned by Cecilia three years ago, when she chose to marry Milo. Of course, she disappointed many a man that day," Addison said. He scratched at the corner of his eye and paused for a while before speaking again. "When I heard that Giles was dead, killed by the trolls, I mourned like any brother. But inwardly I was relieved. I thought we had averted a crisis. Instead we created one far worse. Giles absolutely must *not* become king. But at the moment I can't think of any way to stop him."

Addison leaned back against the leg of the table. "Of course, I have flaws of my own. Arrogance, for one. An overabundance of reserve. And others I'm sure you could point out." A little breath puffed out of Addison's nostrils; it was the closest he'd come to a laugh. "I have not treated you well, Patch. I should have recognized your talent. Because Milo was right about one thing— you *are* clever. So if you have any more ideas, I should like to hear them."

Patch shook his head. "I don't know, my lord. I keep wondering how your brother is getting those monsters to do his will. I believe he discovered something about the trolls, something they don't want anyone to know. I said that to Giles, and you should have seen the look he gave me. It made me sure that I was right."

Addison nodded. "It was probably the same look he would give our father when we were boys and my father confronted Giles with the truth."

"Will Sweeting said we should ask ourselves why the trolls have never come before. And he was right—if they are so invincible, why have they stayed in the Barren Gray? There must be something that keeps them away."

Patch reminded Addison about the things that Griswold had told them, the things that felt like clues ready to piece together. Addison listened with his brow wrinkled, then shrugged. "I don't know what it might be, Patch. But keep thinking. We don't have much time." He stood and tugged at his garments to smooth them. "It is amazing to me that the life of a simple apprentice has become so intertwined with the fate of our kingdom. Perhaps you are meant to solve this puzzle."

Or maybe I was meant to bring disaster down on us all, Patch thought, *like the first rolling stone that triggers a landslide.* They remained there for a while, Patch trying to push that notion out of his head and Addison lost in his own thoughts, until men began shouting outside in the courtyard. The nobleman lifted his head. "What now?" he asked wearily. Patch followed him out of the chapel.

The courtyard was crowded with the refugees from the village, but it was easy to find the source of the noise. Near the gatehouse a group of men stood in a circle, surrounding Mannon and a soldier whom Patch did not recognize. The fight was over by the time Patch got there. Mannon stood over the other man, putting his boot on the wrist that held the sword and bringing his own blade to the soldier's neck.

Addison pushed his way across the courtyard. "Mannon! Don't harm that man—what are you doing?"

Mannon turned, his chest heaving up and down, and shouted back. "I heard him talking to the others, trying to convince them to surrender the king and take Giles's side!"

Addison stood directly over the soldier and stared down. The softening of his features was long gone—it was the same stony face Patch had always known. "Is this true?" Addison asked.

The soldier was on his back, his eyes darting among Addison, Mannon, and the sword at his neck. "What choice do we have? We can't fight the trolls. I heard what they did at Half! Arrows don't kill them. Fire doesn't burn them. We have to give them Milo—and that apprentice!"

"Lock him away," Addison said, jabbing his chin toward a tower at the corner of the castle. A group of men came over, lifted the fellow by the arms, and dragged him off. He screamed over his shoulder at them, nearly in tears, "It's madness to fight! We'll be slaughtered! And I'm not the only one who thinks so!" The frenzied voice died away as the soldier was pulled inside the tower.

Addison turned to face the growing crowd. "Perhaps it is true," he said. "Some of you may think it is hopeless to fight this enemy. Perhaps you think we should bind up our king and that boy"—here Addison pointed toward Patch—"and hand them over to Giles." As he spoke, Addison looked at each man in turn. Some met his glance, others looked at the snowy ground, and others stared nervously at the walls as if the trolls might burst through at any moment.

"I will tell you this," Addison said. "Giles is my brother; no one knows him better than I do. And for my part, I would rather die fighting those trolls tonight than live one day in a kingdom ruled by my brother. By my false, pitiless, diabolical brother."

Addison pointed toward the prison tower. "Who was that man?"

"Doggett," someone replied.

"Doggett, then. Doggett is in the dungeon now. But

consider this—he will be quite lonely in there. Because Milo is not a king who imprisons people for the least offense. How many of you have been treated unjustly? How many have been jailed or whipped without cause? Or seen your friends hang from the gallows, or had every last penny taken from you by the king's taxmen? What, none of you? Well, I can promise you something—if Giles is king, you can expect all of those things. With a king like Giles, Doggett would be in a dungeon so thick with the king's enemies that none could lie down to sleep.

"And this is why I tell you, *no!* We will not surrender Milo. We will not surrender the apprentice. And anyone who desires otherwise will have to pass through me first."

"And me," said Ludowick.

"And me as well," growled Mannon, shouldering his way through to join them.

"And me," shouted a frail, ancient man in the crowd. He was a farmer, sitting in a two-wheeled cart. A few in the crowd shouted their approval.

Addison grabbed Patch's arm and tugged him along as he climbed onto the cart and stood on the bench next to the farmer. "Do you see this boy?" Addison cried out to the buzzing throng. "He is not a soldier. He is not a knight. He is not a lord or a baron. This is Patch, the tailor's apprentice from a town so small you've never heard its name. He stood on a bridge over a fallen friend and killed one of those beasts. *By himself!*" The crowd gasped. Patch gaped out at them, without the smallest idea of how to react. "So the king summoned him to Dartham— and now the mightiest troll lies drowned in the muck at the bottom of the lake! If one boy can fight them, why can't *we* fight them as well?"

The people crowded in close, soldiers and villagers alike. They cheered and shouted Patch's name and reached out to touch his feet.

"We *can* fight them!" Addison shouted on. "With our swords, our spears, our axes, our lances. With our rakes and pitchforks, if we must. Let them come! We'll drop stones on their ugly heads. Let them try! We'll rain boiling oil on their shoulders from the walls. They say a troll at Half took a hundred arrows and survived? Let us see one take two hundred arrows and live!"

The people in the crowd shouted and hopped about with their fists in the air. Some swarmed up the sides of the cart, clapping Patch on the shoulders, tugging at his garments. He smiled as best he could and tried to look brave. Over the heads and arms of the crowd, he saw Simon dancing happily and slapping his hands together high over his head.

Only when the clamor died away a bit did they hear the urgent voice of the constable calling from the top of the wall, "Lord Addison! Lord Addison! Here, sir, you must come here!"

Two of the trolls were tearing one of the low buildings

outside of Dartham apart. The sharp cracks of breaking wood drifted up to the walls of Dartham, muffled by the gathering mist that rose from the snow.

"See there—they are pulling out the largest timbers and leaving the rest," the constable said, pointing. The trolls, each with a dozen heavy beams across his arms, added them to a growing pile. "I don't think they're for burning. Or they'd have brought them to their fire."

"Do you know what they're doing, Lord Addison?" Patch asked. Addison did not answer. He looked at Ludowick, who frowned back at him and took a heavy breath.

"Where is Giles, that snake?" Mannon wondered.

"Haven't seen him since the mist got so thick," the constable said. "He's out there somewhere, though, beyond the range of our arrows. With three of his gang around for protection, I'm sure. Hold on—over there, that Murok is coming."

The marble-skinned troll lumbered out of the mist with an unlit torch in his hand and walked over to the roaring fire the trolls had built. He touched the end of the torch to the flames to light it and strode toward the gatehouse, stopping on the far side of the ditch, across from the raised drawbridge.

Murok glared up at the men through the narrow slits of his helmet, and a long, low, murderous purr rolled up from his throat. He drove the sharp bottom of the torch handle through the snow and ground it into the soil.

Then he straightened up and began to speak. It made the men grimace and wince to hear his rusty, grating voice. "You have until this stops burning. Then you will surrender the king and the boy and leave the castle. Remember—the queen stays. Lash her to the throne." Murok began to walk away, then pointed at the torch again. "Until it goes out. Then the walls come down."

He growled something at the two trolls who had collected the timber. They grabbed the heavy wooden beams and came toward the walls.

"Archers!" Addison called, raising one hand high. Three dozen men stepped to the edge of the wall and pointed their arrows at the approaching beasts.

The trolls stopped on the far side of the moat that surrounded the walls of Dartham, ten feet deep with a bottom of frozen mud. They hissed up at the men along the wall and heaved their timbers into the ditch.

"Do not move, or we will fire," Addison warned. The trolls grinned at one another and leaped into the ditch. "Now!" Addison shouted, and a flock of arrows flew shrilly down.

The trolls were crouched with their backs facing the men, and the arrows clanged off the thick armor that covered their backs and heads. The creatures began to claw at the side of the ditch nearest the castle. Every hard, triangular nail on their huge, dense hands was like a shovel. With fearsome strength, they punched and gouged at the frozen earth, throwing chunks of soil and rock behind them. Another volley of arrows whistled down, seconds after the first. Most clattered off the trolls' armor in random directions, but some stuck in the skin of their arms and legs. The trolls ignored the wounds. They went on clawing and digging, and soon had nearly disappeared into the ground, tunneling quickly toward the walls where the men stood.

"What are they doing?" Patch asked.

"Undermining," Ludowick replied, looking grim. "They'll dig tunnels directly under our stone walls, and use those timbers to prop up the foundation so the walls won't collapse at first. When that torch goes out, they'll set the timbers on fire. And when the timbers burn through, down come the walls."

Murok watched from a distance, smirking. When the two digging trolls disappeared into their hole, he stalked off and vanished in the mist.

"I think it's time to speak to the king," Addison said.

CHAPTER 15

Patch leaned against the wall, staring at the closed door to the great hall. He had followed Addison and Ludowick. But when they arrived, Addison told him to wait outside—not unkindly, but firmly—while they spoke to the king and queen. He suddenly heard a familiar voice singing and looked around for a place to hide.

> "Listen to the cat
> As she prowls around the house
> Till she catches master mouse
> And she leaves him on the mat
> Mew, mew, mew mew mew
> Mew, mew, mew mew mew
> Listen to the bees
> Cause they must be—

Patch!! Hoo ha, it's Patch!"
Too late; Simon had spotted him. The fool had his

enormous wheel of cheese again, and he balanced it on his head as he wandered about alone, singing at the top of his lungs. He ran to Patch, taking careful, mincing steps to keep the cheese from falling. Then he plopped down in front of his friend with his long legs, so flexible that it was painful to watch, pointing in nearly opposite directions. "Have some cheese," he said, holding the wheel under Patch's nose.

Patch looked to the ceiling and chuckled despite his dark mood. "I think I will," he said. He hadn't eaten in a long while, and his stomach was rumbling. He ripped a chunk away from a place that Simon had not yet gnawed and stuffed it in his mouth. "It's delishish," he said, still chewing.

"A gift from the queen," Simon said dreamily, squeezing the cheese against his chest and rocking it like a baby. Patch wished again that he could be as carefree as this simple man, Simon Oddfellow.

"Simon," he said, "is that really your name—I mean the Oddfellow part?"

Simon turned to him with an earnest expression. "That's an interesting story, Patch. For a long time, all I knew was Simon, never the second bit. So I went to this man who was said to be very wise and asked him what my last name was. And he says, 'Well, what family are you from?' And I say, 'I haven't the slightest idea!' And he just looks at me and says, 'You surely are an Oddfellow!' And that's how I learned my name."

Simon took another enormous bite from the wheel and rested contentedly against the wall. Patch struggled not to laugh aloud—but the urge to laugh disappeared quickly when he thought of those trolls digging their way under the walls, carving out in minutes what would take men days.

"What's wrong, Patch?" Simon said, tipping his head sideways.

"I'm afraid of what's going to happen."

"I know how to cheer you up!" Simon cried, putting the cheese aside.

"I'm not squeezing your nose," Patch grumbled.

"No, no, no," said Simon, wiping his hands on his shirt. "I'll draw you pictures. Even the trolls liked this. For a while, anyway. Before they swatted me." A pouch dangled from his belt. Simon untied it and turned it upside down, spilling dirt onto the floor.

"You carry dirt with you?" Patch asked.

"Don't you?" Simon replied, with his brow furrowed. "Anyhow, watch this." The fool spread the dirt in a thin layer across the wooden planks. A tiny stick was hidden in the dirt. He plucked it out and began to draw with its sharpened point.

"First, I always draw a pig," the fool said. And very quickly, he produced a fine picture of a pig.

"You're a good artist, Simon," Patch said.

Simon's face shone, and somehow it made the sadness in Patch deepen. An unspeakable horror was lurking just outside the castle walls, poised to attack, and yet every small pleasure and every compliment gave Simon such joy. *Who's the real fool?* Patch wondered.

"Second, I always draw a cow. . . ."

The door to the great hall opened. Addison was there, and he beckoned Patch to come inside. "Stay here, Simon," Patch said.

"Come back and I'll do more!" Simon called after him.

"Join us," Milo said, and Patch took a seat among the king, the queen, Addison, and Ludowick.

"I thought you should be here, Patch," Milo continued, "since it is you and me that Giles has invited to drink the wine—the poisoned wine. A lesson to all men, I suppose: Beware what tactics you employ, for they may surely be used against you in turn."

Milo leaned forward on the table, clasping and unclasping his hands as he spoke. "We have been arguing in here, my boy. I first proposed to go out and take that drink, if Giles would only allow the rest of you, including Cecilia, to go free."

"Milo, I thought we settled this," Cecilia said sternly. "You will not."

Milo took her hand and held it between his. "Yes, we did settle it. You are right, of course; you often are. If I believed it would serve any purpose, I would take the poison. But that would only put off death and agony for our people, because that will certainly be the result should Giles rule this land. So we will fight them."

"We are not helpless, sire," Addison said. "Not with two hundred men-at-arms, a hundred archers, and a dozen knights. Who can say—we may beat them yet."

"In fact we may," Milo said. "But we must also prepare for the worst. And that is why, my queen, you will not be here when Giles comes for you."

"I am not leaving without you!" the queen cried.

"And *I* thought we settled *this*," Milo replied. "I have listened to your advice for all these years, but this time you will heed mine. I will not surrender you to Giles. And I will not leave this war for others to fight in my place. Ludowick, my friend. You will escort the queen through a little-known door in the eastern wall."

Cecilia closed her eyes and shook her head slowly. Ludowick began to protest, but Addison held up his palm to cut him off. "Ludowick, *the queen must be saved*," Addison said.

"Yes. The queen must be saved," said Milo. "Ludowick, my friend, I know you would rather be here, fighting by our side. But I trust you and need you to do this for me. I pray the fog will keep you hidden from the trolls, and that you may find your way across the river to safety. Go south, to our fortress by the sea. If we are victorious here we will send word. If we are not, the survivors will meet you there. Go now and ready yourselves."

Ludowick stood and took Cecilia's arm, gently pulling. As they left the room, the queen turned and stared at the king, her face a composite of anger, pain, and love.

When the queen and Ludowick were gone, Milo extended a hand to Patch. "Young man, you have an excellent mind. I am glad that we have met."

"As I am, sire," Patch said, taking the hand.

"And it is my wish that you leave Dartham now, as well," Milo said.

"What! Why?"

"Patch, there is no point in your staying here," Milo said. "You're not a warrior. I want you to go. Back to your tailor shop in your little village, far away from all of this. There's no shame in that. Or to our fortress by the sea, if you wish. But you must go. Your swift legs will carry you to safety."

Patch shook his head and his eyes grew hot with tears.

"Come, Patch, don't take it badly. You've been a good friend to the kingdom. Here, I have something for you." Milo produced a purple velvet pouch with a golden drawstring at its throat and laid it on the table before Patch. "Some gold. Some jewels. Not a king's ransom, but it should make you a wealthy man by the standards of your village."

Patch stared at the little sack. "Nothing I tried really worked. There's no reason to reward me," he said quietly.

"Take it anyway," Milo said with a smile. "Less for Giles to plunder." He grasped Patch's wrist, turned the palm up, and put the pouch in Patch's hand.

After what Mannon had said to him in the chapel, it was of little comfort to Patch to find that he had not been hoping for a reward at all. The small fortune in his hand meant nothing to him, and he would have traded it in a moment if Milo would only let him stay.

The king tousled Patch's hair, then turned to Addison. "Goran, you will assume command of our defenses. For my part, I will gladly follow your orders. I will go now and say a proper good-bye to my wife. Meet me by the barracks when you are ready."

"Why don't we all just run, my lord?" Patch said to Addison when the king was gone. "There are too many of them—why should anyone stay, when you know there's no chance?"

Addison smoothed one of his eyebrows. "A few people may be able to slip past them. But a mad rush by hundreds—there would be a slaughter. And besides, we would hand Giles exactly what he wants. Dartham and all the gold in its treasury. And worst of all, the crown. If he is king, I'd rather not live in this kingdom."

"So don't! Live somewhere else."

Addison grunted and leaned back in his chair. "You don't understand, Patch. I have to stay here and fight. If there's even the smallest bit of hope, I have to fight."

"But there is no hope," Patch said, his voice shaking.

"How can you of all people say that! The tailor's apprentice who killed two of these beasts by himself!" Addison shook his head. "If you can fight them, then we can fight them. But it's all about battle and blood-shed now, Patch—there is no more time for tricks and clever plans. That is why it is time for you to leave."

Addison walked to the door through which Patch had entered. He swung it open and said, "Master Simon. Will you come in, please?"

Simon uttered a delighted squeak, seized up his cheese, and marched proudly through the door, raising his knees waist-high with each step. He stopped in front of Patch, grinning happily.

"Simon, you have served the kingdom well," Addison said.

The fool's eyebrows shot up. "I have?"

"Yes. And now the kingdom has one more thing to ask of you."

Simon thrust out his chest. "Anything, my liege."

"I know you are fond of Patch. You owe him your life, after all. Now I ask you to look after him. See that Patch gets safely away from the castle. Knock him silly and carry him if you must."

"I won't go," Patch said, his voice rising to a shout. "If you're staying, so am I!"

There was an odd look on Addison's face as he turned and put his hands on Patch's shoulders. All of the pre-tense and the lordly bearing was stripped away, and here at last Patch could see Addison the man, with an expression that was equal parts anguish and affection. And when Addison spoke, the voice too was different, softer than before. "Patch—very soon the trolls will attack. If you are here, it will not make a difference. But if you get out, it *will* make a difference. At least to me. Even if all else is lost, I'll know that your clever mind is still out there, trying to figure this all out. You keep saying there is some weakness to these trolls, some answer that just manages to elude you. But you'll never find it if you die here tonight."

Patch could not think of a single word to say. Simon watched with his bottom lip clamped between his teeth.

"Remember," said Addison. "The fields to the east seem less heavily guarded. Stay low and don't be seen."

Patch suddenly felt weary. His head drooped and his chin touched his chest. "How do I find the fortress by the sea? I will join the queen there."

"Once you've left the castle, follow the river south, one day's journey on foot. Turn west where the river enters the sea. The fortress is ten miles from there, on a piece of land a hundred feet away from the shore. It can be reached only by bridge or boat, and the bridge can be destroyed if necessary. It is a cold and forbidding place, without the comforts of Dartham. But the queen will be safe there—only we and the king know where Ludowick is taking her."

"I—I just want to get some of my things. My tailor's kit."

"Of course. And if you stop by the kitchen, you will find provisions waiting for you. Then be on your way.

The door you will use is just beyond the vineyards. I hope we meet again, young apprentice. Who knows? Perhaps my garments will need repair after this battle." Patch had to smile—this was the closest Addison had ever come to making a joke.

Simon cleared his throat loudly. "Lord Addison?" he said.

"Yes, Simon."

"I think you're a very brave man."

Addison stared back. "And I don't think you're such a fool after all."

Simon put an arm around Patch and guided him toward the door. "Fancy that," he whispered into Patch's ear. "You give a fellow a compliment, and he turns right around and insults you."

CHAPTER 16

The torch sagged to one side as the snow where it was planted softened in the warming air. Its light was dying. The two trolls who had dug the holes under the castle walls crept close to watch with an eager, hungry look in their quicksilver eyes.

The flame sputtered, and then there was nothing but a thin line of smoke that rose like a serpent's ghost and melded into the thick fog.

The grinning trolls seized up burning logs from their fire and ran toward Dartham. Once again, futile arrows clanged off their armor as they dropped into the moat and crawled into the tunnel. The trolls vanished from sight, but the men above knew what they were doing: setting fire to the wooden beams that held up the walls.

CHAPTER 17

The air was milder than ever, and the fog thicker. Patch and Simon came away from the kitchen with enough bread, cheese, and salted pork to last a week. The vineyards stood before them, and somewhere beyond was the tiny door in the thick wall that they would use to slip out into the fog-shrouded fields.

"Hold on, Simon, I want to hear this," Patch said.

Addison had the knights and soldiers assembled in the courtyard, along with the most able of the villagers. The bowmen listened from the walls above. Their expressions were grim and uncertain; they shifted from foot to foot and looked at one another's faces, trying to see if their anxiety was shared. Patch watched them as Addison continued to call out his instructions. "Knights, do not put on your armor; wear your padding only. Armor will not protect you if you fall into their grasp, and agility is our advantage over these stupid, lumbering beasts. Strike, retreat, and strike again; let us try to exhaust them.

"Men-at-arms, we will use our longest pikes and spears, so you may stab at the trolls while staying out of reach. If you are cornered, brace the end of the shaft against a wall or stone, so that the troll might impale himself when he rushes you. If a troll has fallen, finish him off with axes, maces, and broadswords.

"Archers, we shall direct all our arrows at a single troll at a time. Let us slay one, and see if the rest lose heart. Start with Murok, if he is within range. If not Murok, then choose the largest. Once that troll has fallen, move on to the next largest.

"Tell the men in the winch room to raise the inner portcullis. That's right, *raise* it. But only to let it fall and crush the first troll who breaks through and wanders beneath it.

"You villagers—we are glad to have you. Your hands and arms are strong from your work in the fields of Dartham. And now your strength will serve in its defense. Take your place on the parapet beside the archers, where you will rain death upon the trolls. There are stones for you to hurl. And while fire does them little harm, our pots of quicklime and boiling oil might do the trick.

"Your king will command the village folk. Mannon will direct the archers. And I will command the soldiers."

If Addison had any doubts that they could succeed, he'd hidden them someplace where no one could see. His voice and gaze were steady. Patch saw new confidence blossoming among the assembled men—they nodded, stood taller, clapped one another on the shoulder. A light was in their eyes now, and many were smiling. Patch wondered if it was possible that they could win this battle after all—but his mind kept returning to the towering, powerful trolls, now thirty or more strong.

"Come, Patch," Simon said, tugging at his sleeve. "I promised."

"Do you smell the fire?" Patch asked. He pointed to the smoke, billowing up darker than the fog, rising up outside the wall near the gatehouse. "They're burning the timbers."

Simon sighed and frowned, and tugged again. This time Patch followed. They walked through the vineyard, past the rows of gnarled and leafless vines laced to wooden frames. The eastern wall loomed before them. At its base they saw a slim rectangular opening, six feet high. A soldier was stationed there, and he watched them approach. "Thought it might be you. Remember me?" the soldier asked when they stood before him.

"Sure," Patch said. It was the fellow who'd found him in the middle of the lake.

"Never seen you before," Simon said, rolling his eyes toward the sky and pursing his lips. Patch recalled how rudely the soldier had treated the fool when they met. Not that he blamed him.

"Right through there," the soldier said, pointing at the opening with his thumb. "Quickly now, I'm barring the door after you go."

"Has anyone else been through?" Patch asked.

"Just Sir Ludowick, and a fellow I didn't recognize." Patch nodded. *The queen, in disguise.* He walked through the doorway. As Simon followed, the soldier stretched his arm out to stop him. Simon whimpered like a puppy.

"It's all right," the soldier said. "I just wanted to tell you ... I saw what you done. Running out there and saving that kid from the trolls. While us soldiers stood there too afraid to move."

"Oh," said Simon, with a proud grin spreading on his face. He crossed his arms and leaned back against the wall. "Well, my good fellow ..."

A low roar rose up from the distance, resonating in the ground under their feet. Through the mist Patch could only see the vague shape of the wall across the courtyard. A gap appeared in the middle, and he heard the rumble and thud of the great stones tumbling down.

"The wall," someone shouted. "There goes the wall!"

Overhead came whistling sounds, followed by resounding crashes as boulders were flung at Dartham from the outside. The great rocks exploded on the walls of the castle and shattered tiles on the roofs. The archers bent down to shelter behind the jutting blocks of stone on the wall. Somebody somewhere began to scream for help.

Patch stepped back toward the courtyard, but Simon wrapped his arms around him and pulled him toward the door. "The king ordered us to leave," he shouted at the soldier.

"I know," the soldier shouted. Patch writhed and kicked, but he could not escape Simon's grasp. The soldier shoved the two of them into the opening and down the dark tunnel that passed through the wall. When they reached the ironclad door on the far side, he clapped a hand over Patch's mouth. "If you're trying to sneak out of here, you two might want to shut your mouth," he said into Patch's ear. "Or you'll be troll food for sure. Now hold on."

The soldier peered through a small hole at eye level in the door, shifting left and right to widen his view. "Don't see any of them. They're out there, though—patrolling outside the walls." He slid an enormous bolt back and eased the door open. Ahead of them was the deep ditch that surrounded the castle walls. Across it lay a temporary bridge, just a single narrow plank with no railing. "Over you go," the soldier said. "And good luck to you."

"He wasn't such a bad fellow after all," Simon said. "I should have offered him some cheese."

"Quiet!" barked Patch. There were terrible sounds all around them. They heard grunts and howls of trolls, more screams from the walls above. A roar came from within the walls, and it made Patch shiver despite the growing warmth in the air—at least one of the beasts must have climbed over the fallen rubble into the courtyard of Dartham.

There was a tower not far away. *Ffft, ffft.* Patch heard arrow after arrow fly out from the narrow slits that the archers hid behind. From out of the mist, trolls heaved boulder after boulder at the tower, rocking it and dislodging the stones. The tower would not take this battering for long, Patch could see. *Not long at all.*

Amid all the noise, they heard heavy thumping steps approaching. "Run," Patch whispered. They fled just as an ugly silhouette, twelve feet tall and nine wide, holding what looked like an enormous axe, emerged from the mist.

They dashed across a frozen vegetable field, the snow turning to slush under their feet, and came to a knee-high rock wall. The plodding steps could still be heard—and the pace seemed to have quickened.

"Up on the wall—so we don't leave tracks," Patch said, putting his mouth close to Simon's ear.

"Brilliant!" Simon exalted, clapping his hands.

"Hush!" Patch hissed. Behind them he heard a sound in the fog. The footsteps were coming straight toward them for certain, squishing in the soggy field. The two ran along the wall, making noise only when a loose stone moved under their feet and grumbled against its neighbor. When the wall ended after a few hundred feet, Patch turned to stop Simon, putting a finger to the fool's lips. "Listen."

The footsteps were still out there. The mist made it hard to judge, but the troll no longer seemed to be heading their way. The sound faded. Patch turned to tell Simon that the troll had lost their trail. But Simon was staring up goggle-eyed over Patch's shoulder, and he had thrust his knuckles into his mouth. Patch whirled about. For a brief, terrible moment, he thought he was seeing the largest troll yet, twice the size of any they'd met, with arms spread thirty feet wide—but then he recognized the shape for what it was. He practically fainted with relief and leaned against the fool. "Windmill, Simon. It's a windmill. Come on." They hopped off the wall and ran inside.

Simon stared up at the innards of the mill, at the wooden wheels and gears that would turn the grindstone when the wind turned the sails. "What are we doing here?"

"Thinking." Patch shrugged off his pack and laid it on the stone, which was sprinkled with fine meal. The man who worked the mill had lived here as well; his straw mattress lay in one corner, and the crude table and bench where he took his meals was nearby. Patch sat and crossed his arms.

"Thinking? At a time like this?" Simon said.

Patch bolted upright, knocking the bench over, as they heard a high scream not far away. It was followed by a shout: "Run! I said *run!*"

"It . . . sounded like Ludowick," Patch said, a numbness coming over his brain. *And that scream might have been Cecilia.* "Stay here," he cried.

Patch raced out the door and turned in the direction of the shouts. As he ran, faster now without the heavy pack across his shoulders, he heard the deep voice of a troll somewhere before him: "Gargog! Over here!" And an answering cry, behind him: "Hold on!"

There was a patter of feet, so light compared with the thunderous steps of the trolls, and Patch glimpsed a small figure in the mist, moving stealthily off to his right. He could not risk calling out from this distance, so he ran as quietly as he could toward the person. The closer he drew, the more certain he was that it was the queen, dressed like a stable boy. She disappeared behind a tiny cottage. When Patch rounded the corner to follow, he found himself staring down the length of a sword pointed at his throat. At the far end of the sword he saw Cecilia's face—her eyes wide and fearful, then suddenly relieved to see him. She lowered the sword and rushed forward to embrace him.

"We have to hide," she said, looking toward the door of the cottage. Patch shook his head and took her hand. He led her toward the mill, but stopped when he heard the low, gravelly voices, one just before them and one just behind:

"Where are you, Yurg?"

"Right here, you stupid lump!"

There was a hay wagon nearby, tipped over with its

load of hay spilled on the slushy ground. They pressed themselves against the hidden side just as the two trolls stalked into the clearing. Patch looked at the ground around them. He was relieved to see many sets of footprints that the fleeing peasants had left in the snow—theirs would not stand out among them.

"What was it?" the one called Gargog asked.

"A man. And a woman—might have been the queen. She screamed when she saw me, or I'd have thought it was a boy."

"The queen? Did you catch her?"

"Oaf! Does it look like I caught her?"

"So what happened?"

"The stupid man got in the way. Waved his spear in my face while the woman ran. He took off when I broke the spear—but it's the woman we have to find. She's wearing a brown cloak. She's got to be near here somewhere. I caught her scent—I'll smell her out!"

Patch glanced at the queen. Her lip was curled up in an expression of utter disgust.

"I'll tell you what smells, Yurg. This whole business. Letting a man make slaves of us."

Patch had been waiting for the right moment to dart away with Cecilia, but now he craned his neck, suddenly eager to hear every word.

"You know the game, Gargog," Yurg said. "If we don't obey . . . you know what he'll do. Can't have that, can we?"

"Why not just kill him? Won't that solve the problem?"

"Because, idiot, he said he's not the only one who knows."

"I think he's just saying that—so we don't snap his scrawny neck and make a stew of him."

"You want to take that chance? Hold on!" Yurg began to sniff at the air. Patch risked a peek over the top of the wagon and saw the troll turn his nose to the right and left. He saw Yurg gesture toward the cottage, and Gargog bare his fangs in a smile. They crept—as quietly as such massive creatures could creep—toward the low building.

Patch looked at the queen and whispered, "Get ready." The trolls snarled and began to tear the roof off the cottage. With the sound covering their footsteps, Patch led Cecilia away, keeping the wagon between them and the trolls for a while before turning toward the windmill. Soon the high domed building and its four broad sails loomed before them.

Simon had unpacked what was left of his cheese and was sitting on the large round millstone, munching contentedly away. He grinned as Patch and Cecilia came through the door. "Hello, Patch. Hello, young man."

Patch eased the wooden door shut behind him. "This is the queen, Simon. She's only dressed like a man. Now put that cheese away before the trolls catch a whiff."

Simon looked back and forth at the queen, the cheese,

and the queen and cheese again, utterly baffled. Finally Cecilia took the cheese from his hands and placed it in the pack for him.

"It sounds like Ludowick got away," Patch said.

"Thank goodness for that," Cecilia said. "Those devils! But Patch, why are we here? We were told to flee."

Patch paced across the floor. "We can't, Your Highness! You heard the trolls. Giles knows something about them, it's the only reason they obey him. But what is it? Will Sweeting knew the answer was there. If we can only figure it out . . ." His mind was abuzz with that feeling again, the sensation that the answer was so close. He slammed his fists on the table, and Simon squeaked with surprise. "Think about what we know," Patch said. "The clues. They stick to stony ground. But what does that mean?"

"They can't fly!"

"Simon, don't be—"

"They can't swim!"

"We know that, but that doesn't—"

"They don't like the fields!"

"Well that's—"

"Or the meadows! Or the flowers!"

"But what about the cold?" Patch asked. "They're supposed to prefer the cold. They invaded during winter, after all. But Simon, you said they built a fire to warm their cave—it doesn't make any sense."

"You're right," Cecilia said. She shrugged off the heavy cloak she'd been wearing and draped it across one arm, then took the seat opposite him. She leaned closer and looked into Patch's eyes. "Keep thinking."

Patch rubbed his temples with his fingers. Simon's answers had been ridiculous, of course. But were they really? There was something to what the fool said. *The meadows, the fields . . .* when Patch thought about that again, the answer seemed to swim up closer and closer to the surface. The Barren Gray: Griswold said it was known for its desolation, its lack of vegetation. *No plants, no flowers.*

The humming in his head grew louder still. And Patch began to listen to it, instead of hoping it would go away. And he began to understand what that low hum might be.

"Simon, keep talking," Cecilia said, keeping her eyes on Patch. "What else do we know about them? What did you learn when you were in their cave?"

"They liked my songs!" Simon said, puffing with pride. Then he deflated, adding, "Until they swatted me."

Patch spun on his chair to face Simon. "Sing it. Sing that song, Simon. Not too loud, though."

Simon stood, brushed himself off, and put a finger to his chin, collecting his thoughts. Then he began to bend and unbend his knees, bobbing to some inner rhythm, and sang.

> *"Listen to the hound*
> *'Cause he smells the fox's blood*
> *When he's running through the mud*

And he makes his happy sound
Bark, bark, bark bark bark,
Bark, bark, bark bark bark!
Listen to the cat
As she prowls around the house
Till she catches master mouse
And she leaves him on the mat
Mew, mew, mew mew mew
Mew, mew, mew mew mew
Listen to the bees
'Cause they must be making honey
When they're sounding rather funny
As they buzz about the trees
Bzz, bzz, bzz bzz bzz
Bzz, bzz, bzz bzz bzz . . ."

Simon stopped and stuck his lower lip out. "And that's when one of them swatted me."

Patch felt countless goose bumps sweeping down his arms. He looked toward Cecilia. She was staring at him, her mouth small and tense and her eyes wide.

"Simon," Patch said. "Didn't you say they hit you when you were drawing pictures, too?"

"True," Simon said, looking cross. He rubbed at some remembered bruise on his rump.

"Draw for me what you drew for them," Cecilia said. "Here." She pointed toward the ground meal that was scattered across the grindstone.

"Certainly, my queen!" Simon skipped to the grind-stone. He spread the meal into a fine, wide layer and began to trace shapes with his finger. "First, I always draw a pig." A moment later, the image of a pig had appeared in the meal. Patch and the queen stepped close, on either side of the fool.

Simon used the side of his hand to erase the pig. "Second, I always make a cow. . . ." As Patch and the queen watched, he drew creature after creature: A mouse. A butterfly. A duck. A frog. A deer.

Patch turned toward the small open window that was near them, afraid he might have heard heavy steps. But just as he became aware of it, the sound stopped. Perhaps it was only the distant crash of more stones striking the walls of Dartham.

"And that's when they swatted me! Now I remember!" he heard Simon say.

The humming in Patch's head grew to a roar as he looked down at Simon's drawing. But of course, he finally realized, it wasn't a hum at all.

Patch hopped and danced about the room, as quietly as he could, whirling his arms in every direction, with a mad grin on his face. "That's it, Simon! Oh, that's it!"

Simon sat on the stone with his arms crossed and the corners of his mouth pulled down. "Well," he said, "if you're going to start acting like a fool, what's left for me to do?"

Cecilia took another look at Simon's picture: a tiny

round head on a striped oval body, with wide teardrop wings and a stinger on the bottom.

"A *bee*, Patch? Can it be that simple?"

Patch rushed up and took her hands, the words spilling out of him. "That's why the trolls stay in the Barren Gray—because it's barren! It's why they keep out of the sun, too. And it's why they're here now, while it's cold and snowy. No fields or flowers in the winter, and no bees! Remember Griswold's stories—the little girl in the meadow that the troll wouldn't chase? And the troll who just dropped dead all of a sudden?"

Cecilia nodded. "Years ago . . . there was a boy at Dartham. The cobbler's son. He was stung by a bee . . . died from it, within the hour."

"A lady in Crossfield, same thing," Patch said.

Cecilia squeezed Patch's hands, and her eyes sparkled. "The apiary is not far from here. Not far at all. Do you believe in fate, Simon?"

"Not really," said the fool, scratching at his chin. "I suppose I wasn't meant to."

And then came a splintering crash over their heads, and an enormous gray fist burst through the roof of the mill.

CHAPTER 18

Bits of straw and fragments of wood and wet snow rained into the mill. A coarse voice yelled, "Yurg! I've got them!"

Patch and Simon and Cecilia huddled against the wall of the mill. "Not now," Patch moaned. "Now that we finally know . . ."

Enormous hands, with those nails as hard and thick as shields, pried through the hole and wrenched it open wider. The three of them flattened themselves against the wall where they might not be seen. A glob of the yellow stuff that oozed always from the eyes of the trolls came down and hit the tabletop with a splat. Instantly they could smell that rancid, sick-sweet odor.

The troll put its mouth to the opening. "I know you're in there," the mouth growled, and then it hissed and flicked its pointed tongue. "I hear you. And I *smell* you."

Simon whimpered, and his chest rose and fell like a panicked mouse's. He held his breath for a moment, and then yanked the cloak off Cecilia's arm. He threw it across his own shoulders, pulled the hood close over his head, and opened the door. "Simon, stop!" Patch whispered hoarsely. But the fool leaped outside and ran, screaming in a ridiculous high-pitched voice, "I am the queen! Don't chase me, don't chase me!"

Incredibly, the troll did exactly that. Through the open door, they saw Gargog stomp away after Simon. Ahead of the fool, the other troll charged out of the mist. Simon veered right. His voice cracked even higher, "Leave me alone, you monsters, I'm the queen!"

Patch and Cecilia had one last glimpse of him, with his gangly legs churning, one hand holding the hood in place and the other waving madly over his head. Then he was lost in the whiteness, with the snarling trolls in pursuit.

"I can't believe that worked," Patch said.

"Fooled by the fool. Let us pray he outruns them," Cecilia said. "Now follow me to the apiary."

It took only minutes to get there, but it seemed endless as they crept through the mist, hugging the hedges and cottages to hide from sight, and listening always for the squishing sound of heavy feet. Finally they were standing in front of a wall made of bricks, nearly six feet high and three deep.

"Here," Cecilia said. There were a series of deep recesses like windows in one side of the wall, each of them packed tight with straw. She went to the nearest one and pulled the straw out, revealing what looked like a large basket. It was shaped like a bell, rounded at the top and woven from thick horizontal bands of wicker. Patch had seen its like before, at the beekeeper's home in Crossfield. "A skep," he said, remembering the name the beekeeper used for them.

"That's right," Cecilia said. She pulled the skep out and placed it on the ground. It stood perhaps three feet high. "The straw keeps them safe from the elements during the winter. Let's look inside." She pulled the domed top away and turned it upside down for Patch to see.

Honeycombs, built of countless waxy six-sided shapes, hung from the wicker in irregular rows inside the dome. And packed in the largest gap between the combs was a mass of hundreds upon hundreds of bees, huddled together in a dense and fuzzy orange-brown knot.

"Look, Patch—the warming air is beginning to wake them." And it was. There was a pulse of movement all over the mass of bees. As Patch watched, a few rolled off the outer layer of the pile, apparently dead.

"They huddle around her during the winter. Many sacrifice themselves to keep her warm," said Cecilia softly.

"Her?"

She carefully replaced the top of the skep. "Yes, Patch. In the middle of all those bees is the queen. Don't you see? They're protecting their queen."

Despite the circumstances, despite his fear for the lives of Ludowick and Simon and everyone inside Dartham, Patch had to smile. "Like Lord Addison said.

'The queen must be saved.'" Cecilia blushed and returned his smile.

Patch looked again at the skep. "We have to warm them more, wake them fully."

"The kitchen, Patch—the ovens are always warm. Let us go!"

Patch shook his head. "I'll bring it. You have to hide here—the trolls will be looking for us."

The skin between her brows crinkled as Cecilia glared at him. "Hide here alone? They have my scent, remember—I would be hunted down like a fox. No, I will take my chances with you, Patch Ridling. And besides, if this works, I need to see the look on Giles's face!"

It was like a fever dream, returning to Dartham. The sounds of the struggle grew louder as Patch retraced his steps and they drew closer to the eastern wall. There was a shriek unlike anything he'd ever heard. It could only be a troll in mortal agony, and it gave him hope. But a moment later, there was a long scream from some poor fellow, a scream that seemed to rise up and arc high through the air, and then down again until it ended with a thud on the ground. And amid all this was the endless crashing stone and splintering timber, the shouts of soldiers and archers, the twang of bowstrings and the whine of arrows, and the roars and hisses and laughter of the trolls.

At last they stood at the edge of the moat, across

from the little door in the wall. "How stupid!" Patch cried. The plank across the ditch was gone, of course: The soldier had removed the temporary span after he and Simon left.

"So we cross it anyway," Cecilia said. She climbed down without hesitation, and Patch followed.

"It's not just that," he said. "The door is going to be locked. And I doubt anyone will be there to let us in."

"We'll see," Cecilia said. She reached the bottom, where a sheet of ice lay under a growing puddle of slush, and her feet nearly slipped out beneath her. "Fancy breaking my neck in the moat after all this," she said. She walked sideways across the ice with tiny, cautious steps.

The sense of nightmare grew in Patch's mind as he followed her, holding the precious skep with one arm and taking her hand with the other. Their pace slowed to a crawl.

"The moat is here to slow down attackers," Cecilia explained, nearly losing her balance again.

"It's working, Your Majesty," Patch said. He was more nervous than ever now, keenly aware that if a troll should wander by, they could not hope to escape while trapped on the ice. But finally they reached the other side and scrambled up the slope. Patch went to the door. There was no handle on the outside—it had been built to blend into the wall. He put his fingers through the tiny window and used that to tug, but the door did not budge. "Locked," he said, frowning at Cecilia. Then he peered through the tiny window. "Hello? Anyone there?" he called.

On the other side of the door, someone was sobbing. He got up on his toes to look down and saw a girl sitting there, hugging the knees that were drawn up to her chest. She must have crawled into this place for refuge during the attack.

"Let me," said Cecilia, putting a hand on Patch's shoulder to gently push him to the side. "Hello, child," she said. Patch could not see, but the sobbing was replaced by sniffing. From the smile on Cecilia's face, he knew the girl was looking up at her now.

"I know you're frightened, young lady. I am too. But I think we have a way to defeat the trolls. And you can help. We need to open this door—but I fear the bolt is too heavy for you to move. Would you like to try? You would? That's a fine young girl."

Patch heard the bolt jiggle on the other side. The girl tried three, four, five times. Cecilia watched through the opening, with her bottom lip between her teeth. Then a small, quavering voice came from behind the door. "I can't do it."

Cecilia glanced at Patch and grimaced. "What is your name, little girl?" she said, her eyes beginning to shine with tears.

"Dulcie," she replied.

"Dulcie, I need you to do the bravest thing you've ever done. You need to find someone strong enough to open this door."

The girl gasped. "But the trolls—they're out there!"

Cecilia's voice shook as she spoke, and she closed her eyes and pressed her forehead against the door. "I know, Dulcie. But you must try. Your king needs you. Your queen needs you. And most important, your friends and your family need you."

"All—all right."

Patch put the skep on the ground while he waited, and he listened to the sounds of the battle inside. Men were shouting; he tried in vain to pick out Addison's voice, or Milo's, or even Mannon's. He heard Cecilia whispering, and saw her hands clasped, and knew she was praying for the safety of the tiny girl.

There was a grunt somewhere in the fields behind them, and a sloshing sound. Then a series of squishing steps, heavy feet sinking deep into the slush and mud. The sound grew louder with every beat. He leaned toward Cecilia and whispered in her ear, "Troll coming."

The slippery moat was in front of them, and only the high walls of Dartham at their backs, with nowhere to hide, left or right. "Should we run?" the queen whispered back.

"Don't know," Patch mouthed, straining to determine the source of the sound. He felt a hint of a warm breeze. The fog was changing. It was no longer a dense and uniform sea of white; now as he looked across the eastern fields he could see the insubstantial curtains of vapor wafting from right to left, randomly obscuring and unveiling the features of the landscape.

Something in front of them, dangerously near, sniffed the air. The moving mists revealed what might have been mistaken for a huge boulder, but was instead a troll that was squatting on the far side of the ditch to examine footprints in the snow. He lifted his head to smell the air. Patch felt the queen's arm slide under his, pulling him in close. "Don't move," she said.

The troll sniffed left, swung his head right and sniffed again. Then the ugly head swiveled to face them directly. Patch could just make out the little gray eyes with their black dots in the center. The beast was squinting, trying to focus.

"Get ready to run," Patch said, barely audible.

The troll rose from his crouch, turned around, and trudged into the mist. Neither of them moved for a few seconds, then Cecilia practically fell over onto Patch. He put his hands atop his head and slid them over the length of his face and back up again. He felt a sweet, lightheaded relief, and heard the queen exhale long and deep. "I can't believe I didn't scream," she said. And then she screamed.

The troll charged out of the fog, snarling. He leaped when he reached the far edge of the moat. He seemed to hang in the air forever, suddenly crystal clear now that he was close, and Patch registered countless details—the color of his warty skin, the ten sharp points of his thick fingers, the wide mouth studded with teeth, the tongue wriggling out of a throat big enough to crawl inside, and those hideous too-small eyes with the golden ick streaming down the cheeks. Patch thought for a moment that the leap might carry the beast all the way across the moat, but he fell to the bottom just short of the near side. Then his head rose up and his hands clawed at the edge for purchase.

So abrupt, so startling, so fascinating in its terrible way was the troll's charge that Patch realized they had wasted a precious second frozen to the spot. "This way," he shouted to Cecilia, and began to run, but she clutched at his sleeve and kept him from going.

And then the door in the wall swung open. A gray-whiskered man, a farmer by the look of him, was there, and the little girl Dulcie was behind him, her high squeal drowned out by the roar of the troll. Patch could feel the ground shaking behind him as the troll's legs swung up over the edge of the moat. He followed Cecilia into the passageway and was about to slam the door shut behind him when he saw the forgotten skep on the ground outside, maybe seven feet away.

The troll was on his feet already and coming at them. Patch sprang out the door and landed like a frog by the skep. A darkness fell over him when he scooped it up, and as he took his first step back toward the opening, he could sense from the corner of his eye a vast gray bulk descending, and he knew that the troll had left his feet and was diving at him with his long, long arms reaching. Patch looked into the passage and saw the old man and the girl backing away, and the anguished look in Cecilia's eyes, her mouth shaped to cry, "No!" A calm voice in his head said simply, *Not going to make it*. He pushed the skep out into the air in front of him, and it floated gracefully toward Cecilia's arms.

It all unfolded so slowly, as if the nature of time was altered and he was soaring through air as thick as honey. He was at the threshold when he sensed the massive hand behind him. Some animal instinct told him to leap, and he did. He was into the passageway, but the hand was coming after him, and as he kept running, his feet churning only air, he felt the troll's fingers at his heel, so firm and heavy that he could actually push off and propel himself away, not once but twice. The troll felt him, and clutched at him, and a heavy pointed nail scratched savagely at his knee and sent him tumbling.

Patch tucked his head down and hit the ground shoulder first. He allowed himself to roll forward, and turned to see the hand right behind him, clawing madly. The troll's head was through the threshold, and the arm and the shoulder, but he was too large to come any farther. The monster snarled and spat in frustration. He bunched his fingers into a fist and hammered at the sides of the passage. Chunks of rock and dust began to rain down.

The old farmer was holding Dulcie, and she had seized his beard in one hand and pressed her face to his neck. Cecilia handed Patch the skep and put her arms around them. "Bless you both," she said, kissing the farmer's cheek and the top of the girl's head. "Now Patch, to the kitchen. If we can."

CHAPTER 19

Patch limped to the end of the passageway with Cecilia. The troll's fingernail had torn through his pants and left a gash above his knee, and the pain seared him like fire.

They peered out from the end of the passageway. They could not see far, but they heard the battle still raging.

The kitchen and its warm ovens were just across the vineyard. But a troll was sitting in their path among the hibernating vines. And not just any troll, but the loathsome Gursh, who had come across an ox and, leaving the battle for the moment, brought it to this remote corner of the courtyard to consume it. They heard the bone splintering between Gursh's teeth and smelled the fresh blood.

"Remember him?" Patch asked.

"The one Simon rescued the child from. Vile creature! We'll have to sneak past him," Cecilia said.

Patch looked at Gursh. This troll's mouth was always foaming, but now the froth was pink with blood, and the raw flesh of the ox dribbled down his chin and chest. Gursh looked around as he chewed, as if nervous that he might be caught by the others. "He'll see us," Patch said. "There's no way to get past."

"We can't wait, Patch!"

"I know. Take the skep. And get ready to run for the kitchen. I'll lead him away."

"But your leg—you can't run!"

"Sure I can," Patch said, shrugging off his heavy cloak. And without waiting for another objection, or some queenly order to stay put, he hobbled out toward the vineyard.

For a moment Gursh was huddled over his kill, gnawing. He had taken his armor and helmet off and laid them on the ground at his side to sit in comfort. Patch walked softly past him, thankful he'd gotten this far before drawing the monster's attention. But then Gursh's head came up again. His silver eyes, which seemed to almost glow compared with the dark-gray-and-lichen-colored hide around them, locked onto Patch.

"Hello, Gursh," Patch said, waving. Gursh flung the ox aside and rose up, snarling.

Patch swerved left and right through the trellises in the vineyard, using them to slow Gursh's pursuit. He glanced over his shoulder. Gursh was a few paces behind, swatting the wooden framework out of his path as he ran. Beyond the troll, Patch saw Cecilia running for the kitchen with the skep cradled in her arms. *How long would it take to rouse the bees?* he wondered. He prayed it would not be long, because as he entered the main area of the courtyard and limped through the rapidly thinning fog, he could see that the situation was grim.

Addison's strategies had led to some minor victories. Patch ran past a troll who was sitting with his back to the wall of the chapel, gazing curiously at a long-shafted pike that had been driven deep into his gut. Another troll stomped madly across Patch's path with his arms flailing—he was positively bristling with arrows, and one shot had been downright miraculous, because Patch saw the feathered shaft sticking out from the tiny eye slit in the beast's helmet.

But the losses were great. At a glance Patch could see at least a dozen broken bodies on the ground—archers, soldiers, peasants, and knights among them. And in every corner of the courtyard were the hulking forms of the other trolls. Some were picking up stones to heave at the archers who remained on the walls, bravely popping up here and there to send down more stinging arrows. Patch was sure he heard Mannon shouting out commands, and it was the first time he was glad to hear that rumbling voice.

A gang of trolls was gathered at the front of the keep. The door was bashed in, and one of them had crawled into the opening, only to be forced back by the battle-axes of the men inside. Some of the trolls clambered up the walls of the keep to reach the upper floors.

There was mayhem everywhere, but each troll was engrossed in his own battle and they ignored the hobbling boy—all except Gursh, who drew closer with every step, making awful guttural sounds. Patch ran on, ignoring the flaring pain and looking for a way to escape his pursuer.

To his right Patch saw a crowd of trolls at the barracks. They pried open the timber walls on one side, and the sharp ends of pikes and spears came stabbing out of the hole. The door at the far end opened, and some thirty men, villagers and soldiers together, spilled out, led by Milo. Addison was the last to emerge. The trolls roared after them, and the men turned to face them, lining up with their long pikes facing the monsters.

There was no time to watch that confrontation— Gursh was nearly close enough to snatch him off the ground while he ran. Patch gained a step by ducking under a long cart and coming up on the other side, while Gursh slowed to heave the cart out of his way.

Ahead of him was the gatehouse, and Patch hobbled toward it, remembering Addison's instructions before the attack. The trolls hadn't bothered to smash down the heavy wooden doors of the front gate. Instead, they'd climbed in over the collapsed portion of the wall. *So there is a chance*, Patch thought. But would the men inside the winch room still be there, waiting?

With Gursh snorting right behind him again, he had no other choice. He ran into the passageway, under the raised inner portcullis. He reached a dead end—a short, high tunnel barred at the far side by the massive doors. Patch ran to them and spun around, wincing from the pain in his leg.

Gursh filled the entrance on the other side of the passage, blotting out the misty scene behind him. He leered at Patch, knowing his prey had no place to run, no hole to crawl into. The foam that forever leaked from his mouth had grown to the size of a beard now, and he wiped it away with one forearm. Patch had never heard Gursh speak before; he had only heard coarse beastly sounds from him. But now Gursh pointed at him with one claw-tipped finger and said perhaps the only word he knew: "Eat."

The troll crouched to fit into the passageway and shuffled toward him. Patch screamed, "Now!" and a sound came from the winch room above. Patch recognized the low rumble of a great cylinder rolling and the high pitch of chains spinning madly. The iron-plated portcullis came down, sliding easily through the grooves in the wall, its pointed ends forming a line of seven spears, each as thick as a tree. Gursh hardly had time to look up before it hit him across the shoulders. And even the thick, leathery skin of a troll could not resist the weight and piercing strength of the massive portcullis. The spikes sank deep into his flesh and drove him to the ground.

Patch heard a wild celebration coming from the room

above him. He looked up and saw a face smiling down at him through the hole in the ceiling. "We were just about to give it up—thought one would never come into our trap. But you done it, lad! We got one!"

Patch waved weakly. Through the hole, he saw the soldier stand up and embrace the other men up there, all of them whooping and hopping about.

He had to get to the kitchen now and help Cecilia. But one obstacle remained.

Gursh was not yet dead.

CHAPTER 20

The creature was on his belly, impaled across the back by four of the seven spikes of the portcullis. His head lay sideways on the ground. He stared at Patch, curling his lips back to show every nasty yellow tooth in his horribly wide mouth. The foam that bubbled from the corner of his mouth ran bright red.

The bulk of the troll had kept the portcullis from dropping all the way to the ground. It looked as if there was enough room to crawl under. But those long, dangerous arms could reach across the width of the passage, if Gursh still had the strength. Patch edged along the wall, cautiously advancing. Gursh made no apparent move, but Patch saw those silver eyes narrowing and the long arm drawing back just a bit, and he knew the troll was trying to deceive him into wandering within reach.

"Fine," Patch said. "I'll wait for you to die." He crossed his arms and leaned back against the wall. He tried to act as if the delay did not concern him, but in truth he

214

felt a growing panic inside—he had to get out, in case Cecilia needed his help.

Patch looked over Gursh's prone form and saw Milo and Addison's group running across the courtyard. It seemed to Patch that their number had shrunk a little. Five trolls were in pursuit, and Patch's heart twisted in his chest when he saw more trolls coming at the men from the other direction, cutting off their escape.

Patch stared at Gursh, willing the creature to die soon. Gursh tried to lift his head off the ground, but it dropped again a moment later. The black dots in his silver eyes had been focused on Patch, but now they wandered across the orbs.

Patch took another cautious step forward, but the eyes suddenly revived and locked onto him again. It was no use; he needed to find another way out.

The wooden bar that braced the door was thick and heavy, but he was able to shove it up and out of the way. It fell to the ground with a thud. Patch pulled the door open a crack, and cursed when he saw yet another obstacle immediately before him. How could he have forgotten? "Hey, up there!" he cried, toward the winch-room above.

The stomping and celebrating slowed overhead, and the same happy face peeked down. "What is it, lad?"

"I need you to lift the outer portcullis—just enough for me to crawl under."

"We'll raise it so you can walk tall, troll killer!"

A different set of chains rattled and the portcullis,

groaning, began to rise. Just on the other side was the drawbridge, raised up to form a vertical wall of wood. There was enough room to squeeze his thin body through on one side. Patch looked out into the fields, and his fists tightened as he saw Giles Addison out there, just beyond the range of arrows, with Murok pacing back and forth nearby. *Coward,* Patch thought. The sound of the rising portcullis seemed to have caught Giles's attention. He had been sitting idly on the cask of poisoned wine that he meant for Patch and Milo to drink, but now he stood and directed his gaze Patch's way.

Patch headed for the collapsed portion of the wall. Giles's head was inclined to one side as it turned to follow him.

The undermined wall looked like the entrance to the underworld. The smoke of the smoldering fire still seeped up through the blocks of stones and the mortar, flint, and rubble that once filled the walls. Patch picked his way up and over the pile, back into the courtyard.

He ran as fast as his wounded stride would bear him toward the kitchen. There were urgent cries on the walls above from the archers. Patch glanced up and saw that a troll had somehow climbed to the top of the outer walls and was stalking along the parapet, whipping his club through the air and driving the men before him. Ahead of the archers was the gap where the walls had tumbled down, and nowhere else to run.

Milo and Addison's group faced an equally grave plight. The trolls had spread into a half circle and were driving them toward the wall of the keep. The men walked backward, with their long pikes radiating out like the spokes of a wheel. As Patch hobbled by, he saw the grim look on Milo's face and the resolute glare on Addison's as he called out instructions to the rest. More trolls were coming from other corners of the courtyard to join in the slaughter. One of them, Patch realized with a shudder, was the towering red-brown monster that had killed Gosling.

Patch ignored the mayhem. The kitchen was drawing near and he kept his eye fixed on the door, hoping Cecilia would emerge. He was not even certain she'd made it that far—but he refused to entertain that thought, not after everything they had gone through.

So many fates unknown, Patch thought. Ludowick and Simon, somewhere in the fields, alive or dead. Mannon, last heard bellowing on the wall. And what about all the others Patch had seen and met since he'd arrived at Dartham?

He and the queen nearly collided as he arrived at the kitchen door. Her cheeks were flushed and her wide eyes glittered with hope as she thrust the skep into his arms.

"Oh Patch, *listen*," she said. And he could hear it well: a frantic humming from inside the woven dome. The skep was as warm as a new loaf of bread, and he could feel the tiny insect bodies inside pelting angrily against the walls of straw. Cecilia had stuffed a rag into the hole at the base of the skep that the bees used to enter and leave their hive.

"Pray it works," Patch shouted, and he ran back toward the trapped group of men.

The trolls could have killed them by now, Patch realized as he came closer, but the soulless creatures were taunting their prey first. They tightened the circle, laughing and jeering. The soldiers and peasants stabbed at them, but the trolls reached out and plucked the pikes from their grasps one by one and snapped the shafts over their knees. Addison had lost his spear and had drawn his sword. Some of the men began to weep.

"Hey, you devils!" Patch shouted. A few of the trolls turned to look, and one of them stepped away from the rest, wielding a heavy club. It was the red-brown troll, Patch was pleased to see, coming at him with that chilling smile on his face. It was the same smile that had horrified Ludowick on the day that Gosling fell, a smile with one long fang jutting crookedly from the corner of his mouth. Patch pulled the top off the skep and hurled it toward the beast.

It was only a guess, Patch thought, watching the skep break into two separate halves and tumble at the troll's feet. *A guess built on meager evidence, the word of a fool, and a leap of faith.* He could very well be wrong.

The troll looked down, not recognizing this thing, puzzled by what danger such a flimsy object could hold. As the pieces of the skep rolled to a stop, the bees flew up, lazily at first in the mild air. The troll saw them. His eyes seemed to double in size. Patch heard him gasp and watched him go rigid, paralyzed with fear for a fatal moment.

The bees sensed something, because a humming cloud of them rose toward the troll's head. At first they spiraled up slowly, but as they neared his face, they suddenly sped arrow-straight toward the troll's eyes. The beast screamed and slapped his head with both hands. A hundred more of the insects flew from the skep, swarming upward. The troll staggered and dropped to his knees in front of Patch, and now he could see through the madly slapping hands that dozens of the bees were writhing in the yellow ooze at the corner of his eyes. *That horrible sweet smell,* Patch thought. *It's drawing the bees in, driving them mad. . . .*

The bees were in a frenzy now, and some disappeared into the troll's nostrils and mouth. The troll howled all the while, a more terrified and high-pitched shriek than seemed possible from such a mighty creature.

And then there was a strange silence at Dartham. Every troll—those in the courtyard, those climbing up the keep, those on the parapet—heard the shrieks and knew something was wrong. They turned to stare at the death throes of the mud-red troll. Even the knights and soldiers and archers turned to look, as the dying troll crumpled to the dirt with a swarm of bees still orbiting its ugly head.

Patch turned to the circle of trolls, pointed a finger at them, and shouted, "You're next!"

And the ground rumbled as the trolls fled, shrieking with fear. They ran across the courtyard and over the smoking tumble of rocks, climbing across each other when one of them fell in his haste. The trolls that surrounded Milo and Addison's men went by first, and then the rest of them, climbing down from the walls and crawling out from the holes they had punched in the keep and the other buildings.

It was quiet again for just a moment. Then the men who'd been trapped against the wall rushed at Patch, and more people spilled out of the keep and ran down from the walls. They surrounded him and pounded him on the shoulders.

Then a tall man with a great smile pushed through the crowd. It took a moment for Patch to recognize him, but that smiling face belonged to Lord Addison. Addison laughed and seized Patch and lifted him high, and a hundred jubilant people shouted, "Troll killer! Troll killer!"

Cecilia ran up, and she and Patch breathlessly told the king what had happened as soldiers, knights, and villagers alike strained to hear every word.

A rumbling, familiar voice shouted, "Your Highness! Your Highness!" And the crowd parted to let a filthy, exhausted Mannon approach the king. "I was on the walls—thought you'd want to know about Giles," he said.

"Of course—where is he? We can't let him escape."

Mannon snorted. "No chance of that, sire. Murok was out there, keeping Giles safe. When the trolls came running out like chickens, Murok ran off as well. Except he made a point of stepping on Giles along the way. And then a few of the others trod on him for good measure."

Milo shook his head and smiled grimly.

"Er—what did happen? What scared the trolls off?" Mannon asked. He looked at the prone form of the mud-red troll.

"Ask the apprentice. He's the one who did it," Addison replied, gesturing toward Patch. Mannon seemed to wince as he turned toward Patch with his eyebrows raised.

"Bees," Patch said, grinning.

"Bees, eh?" Mannon said. He scratched at his beard. "Well, good work, Patch. Always knew you had it in you."

The Brave Apprentice

"Of course—where is he? We called him, and—"
Murron shouted. No glance of that, in a Murdeva
murdered, leaping like a sly. When the bells came ringing out—

—made—

hum less of crowd of it parted ground because—
He shook his head and stared grimly.

"He—what did happen? What eaten the well—"
Murron asked. He looked at may peace from clean
touched well—

CHAPTER 21

Patch stood at last at the lip of a pit, in a cavern in the Barren Gray. The summer air was warm outside, but in the heart of this mountain it was cool and dry. A handful of men stood behind him. They were a curious band, all dressed in garments with broad horizontal stripes of orange and black. Their clothes had been stitched with care by a prosperous tailor from the village of Crossfield. And all of the men bore shields with the same emblem: the silhouette of a bee, with broad wings and a stinger jutting from its bottom with a teardrop of venom at the tip, against a background of yellow-brown interlocking octagons.

Patch—or Sir Patryck the Brave Apprentice, as the king had knighted him—held a large box in his hand, a simple wood-framed cube with a handle on top and thin white fabric stretched across its sides.

Directly before them, broad stairs were hewn into the stone, leading to the pit. Each step was as high as a man's

chest. Down there, just beyond the reach of their torch-
light, dark shapes moved among the shadows. There was a
new sound here as well, a wailing, high-pitched and wanting, from perhaps a dozen separate sources in the gloom.

Patch tossed his torch into the pit. It fell like a comet
through the dark and clattered onto the flat stone bottom. Some of the men gasped when they saw the creatures nearby—naked infant trolls that crawled away
from the light, screeching with their eyes squeezed shut.

"The Cradle of Trolls," Lord Addison said.

"Finally," grumbled Mannon.

Another, much larger shape skirted the light of the
flame and crept toward the stairs, climbing with its
hands as well as its feet, as stealthily as its bulk would
allow. As it rose toward the men, its pale face came into
the light, and Patch saw the first she-troll any man had
seen for ages: as tall as the males but even thicker, with
sharp daggers for fingernails instead of shovels, and
tangled, filthy hair that swept the ground as she
crouched.

"That," Patch said, "is close enough. Stop where you
are, or I may drop this fragile package." He shook the
box, and from inside came the angry drone of bees. The
she-troll stopped. Her lips curled back from her fangs
and she hissed.

"I want you to understand something!" Patch shouted.
His voice echoed back from the depths of the pit. "The
days of trolls prowling in the lands of men are over. We

have found your weakness, and the word has been sent forth. Now everyone knows." The pit was silent. Many pairs of baleful silver eyes watched from below.

"If any troll ever again plagues the kingdom, we will unleash a storm of bees upon you. Now even our arrows are dipped in their venom."

At a signal from Ludowick, archers stepped forward and pulled back the strings of their bows, with arrows pointing into the pit.

Patch's voice rose. "Do you understand?"

A reply came from below, high-pitched and shrill. "Very well," it said.

"Then we have met for the last time. Remember what we have said. Stay in your holes in your mountains. Or you will feel our sting. Farewell!"

As they turned to go, an odd-looking man, tall and gangly with wild tufts of straw-blond hair jutting from under his helmet, danced to the edge of the pit. He reached into the pouch at his side. "I almost forgot—we have a gift for you." He put a jar down at the top of the stairs. "Honey, from the royal hives. Queen Cecilia hopes you like it! Hoo ha!" And then the Prince of Fools capered away, flapping his arms and laughing, joining the rest of the brave party.

Turn the page for a sneak peek at
P. W. Catanese's next page-turner!

The Eye of the Warlock

Available Fall 2005

How much sunlight is left? Rudi asked himself. *An hour or two, maybe.* He ran down the wooded path, wondering where the girls might be. After a while, he stopped and shouted their names, but the only answer came from the birds that were startled into flight and the tiny unseen creatures that scurried in the brush.

Farther in, Rudi decided. Agnes wasn't kind, and she was clever. She would have lured the girls deep into the forest, where they'd have no chance to find their way home. *Just like what happened to—what were their names? Hansel. That was the boy. And his sister was Gretel.* They were relatives of his who lived in the same house many years ago. One day they'd been taken into the woods and told to wait by the fire for their mother and father to get them when their work was done. But their parents never came. And then it began to get dark. *Like it is right now.*

He shouted again and put his hands behind his ears to listen. For a moment, he thought he heard something. But no, it was only an owl's cry.

Rudi ran farther and came to a stream with footprints in the muddy bank. There were two small pairs of prints among them, and they pointed in only one direction: deeper into the woods. He leaped across the water and ran on, looking left and right for a place where Agnes might have led the girls off the trail.

He stopped at last and leaned against a tree, hugging his stomach and drawing air into his aching lungs. When he could breathe more easily again he shouted, "Lucie! Elsebeth!"

He heard nothing. But he smelled something. He tilted his head back and inhaled deeply, turned to where the scent was strongest, and sniffed again.

A fire. Somewhere ahead. Rudi stepped off the trail, keenly aware of how easy it would be to get lost. He'd be walking away from the setting sun, so he could find the trail again by heading back toward it, obviously. Or later, by keeping the North Star to his right. He smacked his fist against his thigh. Why hadn't he taught the girls how to find their way through the woods? There were so many things he knew and never shared.

The smoky scent grew stronger as he trotted east, with his shadow stretching long and thin before him. He called again and again, but still no one answered. *Maybe they're asleep by the fire,* he tried to reassure himself. He saw smoke through the trees and sprinted the rest of the way, until he stood in a clearing with the smoldering embers in front of him. But the girls were not there.

Rudi noticed something on the ground near the embers. It was a wreath made from wild vines twisted together. Lucie and Elsebeth surely made it; it was the sort of thing they would do to pass the time. Rudi picked it up and clutched it against his chest. He shouted their names again and again in every direction, until his throat was raw and his voice grew weak.

"No," he moaned. He kicked at the embers, and sparks flew toward the dimming sky. They were out there somewhere, sweet Lucie and serious Elsie, only six and seven years old. But which way? He was no hunter who could track their steps through the woods, reading the trodden grass or broken stems or other subtle signs. Besides, it would be too dark to see anything at all before long. He thought of them lost among the trees, holding on to one another in the black of night, and fought to push that image from his mind.

There was one thing he could do: build up the fire again, until it roared so high it could be seen for miles in the night. *Yes, they'll see it and come back,* he thought. He gathered twigs and sticks and piled them on the embers—it would be easier than starting a new fire with his flint and steel.

The bits of wood smoldered and burst into flame under his coaxing breath, and soon a modest fire blazed again. He needed more fuel now, the biggest, driest branches he could find. At the edge of the clearing lay a dead branch jutting from the trunk of a tree. He seized it and wrenched it off, grunting through his clenched teeth. The branch was long, and he stomped on it to break it into smaller pieces. Somehow it felt good to break it, and he wanted to go on stomping until only sawdust was left and keep on stomping until the whole forest lay in splinters.

"How could they do this?" he screamed. It occurred to him that people could be far crueler than he'd ever believed possible. A raw and powerful kind of anger roared inside him. He was hardly aware that he'd picked up a broken length of the dead limb and was smashing it against the tree, sending chips and bits of bark flying. And then he heard a voice from the shadows.

"Are you looking for the girls?" It was a strange voice, thin and reedy and high.

Rudi froze. He could suddenly hear the thump of his heart inside his ears. It was almost night now, and more light came from the fire than the sky. Between the trees, he spied a pale spectral face with dark eyes staring back.

The voice came again. "I said, are you looking for the girls?"

Rudi had to swallow before he could answer. "Who is that? Who are you?"

The face vanished behind a thick tree and came out on the other side, a little closer. It seemed to float among the shadows. "You are Rudi, aren't you? They said you would come."

"Where are the girls? If you have them, let them go." Rudi opened the top of his bag and drew out a little ax.

"Put that away. Don't be afraid. The girls are safe."

"I'm not afraid," Rudi shouted, but his brittle voice betrayed him. "You say the girls are safe? Then take me to them—please! But who are you? Why won't you let me see you?" He squeezed the handle of the ax to stop it from shaking.

The pale face hung in the shadows for a moment, and then bone white hands reached up and drew a hood over the head. The stranger stepped into the orange light of the fire. It was a woman, Rudi realized; he could tell from the way she moved and her slender hands, and he should have known already from her voice—it was hoarse, but still a woman's. Her head was bowed, so that the hood concealed her features. She wore a long cloak made of deerskin-dyed dark brown, almost black. In one hand she held a bow, and he saw the feathered ends of a bouquet of arrows over her shoulder. Rudi lowered the ax to his side.

"My name is Marusch. Now come. We should leave this place," she said.

"Why? I'm not going anywhere until you show your face!"

"Ill-mannered boy. You may regret what you've asked," she said. The pale, long-fingered hands rose again and pushed the hood back.

Rudi gasped. He couldn't help it. Only the long brown hair that hung past her shoulders in braids seemed normal. Everything else was wrong. Her skin was pure white, as if the sun never touched it. Coarse but sparse hair sprouted all over her face, even her forehead. And her mouth was the worst of all. The lips were shriveled and drawn back, baring a mouth full of long, red-stained teeth.

"Get away," Rudi whined. He stepped backward and raised his ax to ward off the ghastly stranger.

"I warned you," she said. "But now you must . . ." Her voice trailed off and she looked past Rudi. A sound was approaching: footsteps in the woods.

"Lucie? Elsie?" Rudi called out weakly. It was more a question than a hail.

"It isn't them," Marusch whispered. "It was a mistake to build the fire again —now follow me!" Without waiting for a reply, she turned and hastened into the trees. Rudi paused for a moment and listened with failing courage to the approaching footsteps. They were too heavy and too many to belong to the girls. And something was wrong with the sound, somehow. Something unlike the steps of men. Rudi thought he heard other, unsettling, noises mingled with the steps: sounds like hissing and gurgling.

Before whatever it was entered the clearing and saw him, Rudi snatched up his pack and ran after Marusch. In the dim light, he could just make out her form. "Slow down," he called as loudly as he dared. She stopped and waited, then gestured for him to join her behind a fallen tree. She tapped a finger against her drawn-back lips. They hid quietly, and she peered over the top of the log every now and then.

"It is safe," she said finally.

"Who were they?"

"Strange beings that have begun to prowl these woods," she replied. "Now come." And she was on the move again, darting through the trees.

Available Fall 2005